Providence Island

Providence Island

GREGOR ROBINSON

DUNDURN PRESS
TORONTO

Editor: Michael Carroll
Copy Editor: Jennifer McKnight
Design: Courtney Horner
Printer: Marquis

Library and Archives Canada Cataloguing in Publication

Robinson, Gregor
     Providence Island / by Gregor Robinson.

Issued also in an electronic format.
ISBN 978-1-55488-771-2

     I. Title.

PS8585.O351625P76 2011   C813'.54   C2010-902455-9

1   2   3   4   5   15   14   13   12   11

We acknowledge the support of the **Canada Council for the Arts** and the **Ontario Arts Council** for our publishing program. We also acknowledge the financial support of the **Government of Canada** through the **Canada Book Fund** and **Livres Canada Books**, and the **Government of Ontario** through the **Ontario Book Publishers Tax Credit** program, and the **Ontario Media Development Corporation**.

Care has been taken to trace the ownership of copyright material used in this book. The author and the publisher welcome any information enabling them to rectify any references or credits in subsequent editions.

J. Kirk Howard, President

Printed and bound in Canada.
www.dundurn.com

Dundurn Press	Gazelle Book Services Limited	Dundurn Press
3 Church Street, Suite 500	White Cross Mills	2250 Military Road
Toronto, Ontario, Canada	High Town, Lancaster, England	Tonawanda, NY
M5E 1M2	LA1 4XS	U.S.A. 14150

For Linda

When I was a boy, I played with imaginary people and feared haunted places. The people were a father and mother and children — always lots of children — whose parts were played by the stuffed animals in my room: dogs and lions and wolves.

Outside my bedroom window, my real parents would talk quietly below, snatches of conversation and the clink of the ice in their drinks wafting up from the stone terrace. I thought of my father as remote, even austere. My mother was nervous (*highly strung*, people said).

I was an only child. I imagined noisy gatherings, parades, and games in a rambling house with lawns and gardens: a green paradise, far from the woods and ravines and lonesome swamps that haunted my dreams. Especially the swamps, the wide, ragged marshes, the stinking muskeg where there was nowhere to hide, and the abandoned railway line, and that awful swamp: *And when she could no longer hide him, she took for him an ark of bulrushes, and daubed it with slime and with pitch, and put the child in; and she laid it in the flags by the river's brink.*

PART I

| CHAPTER 1 |

I came home to bury my father and to see the big house on Providence Island for the last time. The Millers' house. I supposed it was because I had no family of my own and was an only child that I was so interested in the families of other people. Or perhaps it was atonement — if you believed in that sort of thing. If you thought it meant anything other than regret.

My father and I were "the last of the Carriers," as he used to put it. The Millers, on the other hand, were everywhere, even Hollywood and the United States Senate. How was it that families like theirs kept going, generation after generation, always with money, and even a certain noxious fame? I was beginning to agree with my father: he'd always said that it was because they were corrupt.

I was driving back to Ketchum, Idaho, when my aunt called with the news. She had waited a day before phoning — no doubt meaning to teach me a lesson of some sort (we were Presbyterian), although she had already mailed her letter, she said.

The evening sky was mauve. The plains were patchy with snow between the sage and tumbleweed. My truck was a cocoon on the empty highway.

"Dead?" I asked.

The dials on the dashboard shone green.

My aunt had moved to the village of Merrick Bay to look after my father after his second heart attack, almost ten years before. Her move was a rebuke of sorts, since I would not come home.

Her letter was full of the details of my father's last days. The lakes were the lowest they had been in years. The weather had been fine all fall and exceptionally dry through the winter; there had been little runoff from the forests when the warm weather came. What water there had been was needed in the Musquash to keep the turbines turning; engineers in the capital made those decisions; the integrity of the local electricity system and the flows to the lower lakes were more important than the life of those small resort towns, fading in the off-season.

My father, out for his morning stroll to Ault's General Store to pick up the morning papers, turned and walked out from the shore, through the dead cattails, and into the sucking muck of the bottom of the bay that was usually covered by water. He walked beyond, into the dirty waves, as though hypnotized. I imagine the sky as grey and cold, a glazed look in my father's eye. He stopped dead in his tracks, the water slurping about his ankles, pulling at his grey woollen pants.

A boy from the hotel noticed him: my father was looking at something, something skeletal. He was pointing.

He had spotted the gunwales of the boat the Millers had used to haul garbage to the mainland once a week before they removed the engine and it became just an unwieldy, beamy rowboat. The green rowboat. It had been a leaky wreck even before the "disappearance" of John D. Miller.

My father and the boy from the hotel pulled the boat free. They dragged it, some of the ribs by then disintegrating, along the mud of the lake bottom to the mouth of Sucker Creek.

I see my father as he pauses to wipe his brow and catch his breath. He is panting and pale. He replaces the white handkerchief in his breast pocket and lies down in the damp new grass ...

There he had the heart attack, the third and last of his life.

In the morning Katie and I made love. Afterward, I got up early to help her with the hay.

"This is a first," she said, "you helping with the horses."

Katie boarded horses. She ran river-rafting expeditions during the summer. It was how we had met, after my marriage ended and I moved west. We had been together for almost two years. On and off, as Katie would say.

"I've come across men like you before — men who don't want to get involved," she would say.

"I'm involved with you," I said.

"How do you feel about children?"

"They grow up and turn out to be like the rest of us."

"I meant do you *want* children?" she asked.

I didn't know what I wanted. The notion of children remained to me a fearful swamp.

After breakfast she drove me to the airport. A company plane would take me as far as Salt Lake City where I would transfer to a regular flight for Toronto.

The terminal smelled of kerosene.

"I love the smell of jet fuel," she said.

We walked toward the row of private jets lined up on the tarmac.

"Will you be seeing that woman?" she asked.

"That woman?"

"That rich one you used to talk about."

"That was twenty-five years ago."

She shrugged.

"It's just about my father, his funeral," I said. "The way he died."

"I wonder if you'll be back."

"Room and board," I said.

"How do you get rid of a cockroach?"

"Ask for a commitment," I said.

You could tell from the way she strode away that she was annoyed. We were friends who had become more. She wanted an answer.

"Katie," I called across the tarmac from the stairs to the plane. She turned and gazed at me from the open door of the terminal. "I'll be back." She couldn't hear, but it seemed important. I yelled over the rising whine of jet engines. "I'll be back."

She shrugged, turned, and was gone.

On the flight from Salt Lake City, I dreamed of rattlesnakes in the cracked, dry mud of the pump house at the Applewoods' farm. Marjorie Applewood's warm hands on my neck while she whispers poetry and sex, her breath hot in my ear.

I saw my parents golfing on a sunny afternoon at the Bellisle Club, the lake behind them sparkling like cut glass, my father thirty years younger — younger than I am now.

If it was true that a person didn't grow up until his parents died, did it follow that the loss of one parent left you suspended in a state of arrested development? My mother had been flying to Montreal for her twenty-fifth university reunion. Taking off, the plane failed to become airborne. The pilot tried to abort, but the plane hurtled off the end of the runway, skidded down a ravine, and burst into flames. I was twelve years old. In the pictures in my head, instead of burning, the plane would hit the ground and shatter like a china cup. People used to ask me: what was it like having your mother die when you were so young? The main thing was: nobody hugged you anymore.

I turned forty two months before my father's funeral.

The flight attendant touched my shoulder; we were making our final approach. I buckled my seat belt.

| CHAPTER 2 |

"Ray Carrier, you're back!" said Mrs. Ault. And you still smoke."

"Only at weddings and funerals," I said.

"And between meals."

I handed her my cash — strangely coloured Canadian bills. She took my money from the counter and handed me my cigarettes. My father used to say that Mrs. Ault was the Greek chorus of Merrick Bay.

Merrick Bay was the village at the bottom of the swampy inlet that serviced the resort community of Bellisle out on the point. Bellisle was attached to the mainland by a narrow causeway. There was a clubhouse, the golf course, an aging resort hotel, immense summer houses, and the green islands to the west. Those farthest out had expansive views down the lake. They had names like Greatview, Westwind, The Pines, Blackwood Island, Providence Island.

"Are you alone?" asked Mrs. Ault.

They knew of my failed first marriage and they appeared to know, in Merrick Bay, that I was with Katie.

"We were sorry to hear about your father," said Mrs. Ault. "What could have come over him, walking out into the lake, a cold day like that?"

She pulled her fleece jacket tighter around her, even though outside the sun was shining. In less than two weeks, the May long weekend would mark the start of the summer season for the businesses of Merrick Bay. It was what they waited for all winter.

"I can't imagine," I said.

"That stupid boat," said Mrs. Ault, answering her own question, "that's what." She paused to hear if I would say more, then asked, "You'll be staying up at the house?"

The car I had picked up at the airport was ill-suited to the roads of Merrick Bay. Every winter they grew worse, cracked and buckled by the weather, and every spring the municipality repaired them as best they could. Now they were a patchwork of colours and textures. But with the rise in property values and new development, attention was being paid to what the government called "northern regional infrastructure."

After J.D. Miller drowned and the Millers began their withdrawal from Bellisle, speculators and land developers started filling in the swamp at the mouth of Sucker Creek. Over the years, they moved farther along the creek until the Ministry of Natural Resources finally put a stop to the destruction of what they had started to call wetlands rather than swamp. Where Phil Havelock and I used to set minnow traps in the bulrushes there were now big yellow bulldozers parked on mud flats. Farther back from the creek, there were a couple of new streets of small, concrete-block houses with squat air-conditioning units beside the front doors. The people who lived in these houses commuted to Iron Falls where an auto parts company had built a plant.

When we first came to Merrick Bay, my father would take me to the Government Wharf or up to one of the outcrops behind the house, where granite broke through the thin soil, to look for the Northern Lights. In August the sky would be ablaze with shooting stars — invisible at home, in the city's electric buzz. We would gaze over the line of the forests, the low hills rising in the distance. You could go north from here without meeting another soul, my father said. No lights, few roads, nothing but the dark forest and shambling beasts, the trickle of water into nameless lakes and muskeg, the sighing of the trees. Eventually the stunted pines, tundra, snow, and ice, the cold black water of Hudson Bay, and the Arctic Ocean.

"We are standing at the very edge of the North," my father would say. "The last wilderness."

A century earlier, when the Havelocks and the Applewoods and the other settlers who had received acreage under the Free Grant Lands Act — while they were clearing and trying to farm the hopeless land — rich families from the south were already buying the islands, distant green forests in the lake. Mr. Havelock would tell us how, as a boy, he would accompany his own father as he walked twenty miles with grain on his back to be ground to flour at Iron Mills. At the same time, a few miles away, steamers loaded with materials and equipment that had come by rail from the south were unloading along the shore and on the islands, for the building of elaborate summer cottages, designed by the likes of E.J. Lennox, or McKim, Mead, and White from New York City. People used to take the train to the foot of the lakes then a steamer up to their cottages. By 1910 the Millers had their own steam yacht, *Hiawatha*, at Providence Island. It had been built in Glasgow, disassembled, and shipped out in parts.

My father's house was over half a mile from the lake. It had been remote until the highway went through. The place had been one of the original settlers' farmsteads, but aspen, hawthorn, sumac, and birch had long since reclaimed the fields; even the tops of some slender white pines had started to appear above the new green forest. People from the city were always surprised: why come to Merrick Bay and not have a house on the lake? But my father said that we could see the lake from the attic windows, and if you wanted to, you could always take the yellow canoe and paddle down the creek to the lake. Paddle your own canoe. A rule to live by. Although he was himself afraid of the water and took to a boat of any kind with trepidation. The real reason he had bought a house away from the lake: to him, it didn't make much difference.

My father had acquired the house at Merrick Bay in an estate sale through one of his partners. We didn't use it much at first, perhaps a week of holidays and a few weekends. My mother refused to stay there alone during the week; she had always been nervous, and she said that she didn't know anyone there — that we were part of neither Merrick Bay nor the summer community. After she died, my father decided I should spend more time at the lake. He invited my mother's elder sister, Aunt Beth, to spend the summers with us there. Someone had told him this would be good for me. He once went so far as to take an extra week of holidays himself, but he spent most of his time reading the papers on the porch, tending the garden, and fiddling with the radio, trying to get the opera.

When the house came into view, I saw my aunt standing on the front verandah. She and the house were both smaller than I remembered. She wore one of her generic flowered dresses and a faded blue cardigan. A few strands of white hair blew across her face in the breeze. She was waiting. No doubt Mrs. Ault had already phoned. I parked the car by the weathered posts that marked the edge of the vegetable garden, now overgrown, and carried my suitcase up the front steps. The smell of the poplar trees carried me back.

Aunt Beth gave me a peck on the cheek. "You're in the front room upstairs."

I said I'd be fine with my old bedroom at the back, on the ground floor. (I used to be able to sneak out the window onto the back porch.)

"We always put guests in the front rooms," Aunt Beth said. She turned to open the door for me. She was in her mid-eighties, almost fifteen years older than my father, but she still moved quickly. She was short and getting shorter, and she walked with a slight stoop. "I've made some good thick soup. You go up and wash your hands."

I recognized the creaking in the floorboards as I carried my suitcase up the stairs, and the smell of Aunt Beth's bathroom soap — Yardley's Lavender. In the guest room there was a pair of pictures in matching silver frames on the bureau: my mother and father, myself as a boy.

After my mother died, my father hired a housekeeper, Mrs. Ireland, who worked half days, two hours in the morning and two in the afternoon. He also took me out of the public school I'd been attending and sent me to St. Jerome's. He had the idea that they took their teaching more seriously in the Catholic schools — they did it because it was a vocation, he said, and not for the pensions and the long summer holidays — and he liked the discipline. But the main reason I was sent to St. Jerome's was that the school days were longer there. They kept you busy after class: in the fall, soccer and football; in the winter, hockey and basketball; and in the spring, track, tennis, and baseball. With the exception of hockey — St. Jerome's regularly lost players to Junior A — the priests didn't take sports too seriously, which was just as well for me. I was weak at hockey and football, and took to tennis by default; I had a backhand, could run down any ball, and they let me play indoors year-round. There were other activities — drama, art, chess, the lit club — so that by the time I stepped through the front door at home it was often close to six o'clock, and dark.

Mrs. Ireland would make dinner before she left for the day; there were always casseroles and meats in the refrigerator. At seven, my father would come home. He would drink two whiskies, read the evening paper, and then call me downstairs for dinner.

We would sit in the panelled dining room, under the pale light of the chandelier, my father's cutlery clattering against the china. He chewed his melba toast with noisy vigour. It was a relief to both of us when I excused myself to clear the dishes. After dinner my father read in the upstairs den. In the years following my mother's death he read the whole of Dickens and Scott.

On Fridays or Saturdays he was often out for dinner, sometimes almost the whole weekend. He had woman friends about whom he was pathologically discreet. When I went away to college, he began a long-term relationship with an Englishwoman, a Mrs. Harris. My aunt had told me that whenever Mrs. Harris was in Toronto she would stay at our house. My aunt did not see this in a romantic light. She said that Mrs. Harris was a freeloader.

My father would likely have married Mrs. Harris had she not insisted on living in the country, though nowhere near Merrick Bay; she had in mind something more genteel: horse country. They saw each other several times a year but, by that time, in an ironic turn of events, my father was living in the country with another elderly woman.

On the bureaus of the guest room, I noticed a photograph of my father and J.D. Miller on the front steps of the Bellisle Golf and Yacht Club, J.D. wearing tweed plus fours, his arm around my father. My father was not one for hugging. None of the Carriers are. To the left is the fender of J.D.'s antique Packard limousine. And to the right, standing behind J.D., Mrs. Applewood in her nurse's skirt, a dark raincoat over top, her hands crossed in front.

When I was a boy, my father used to tell me — admonish me, really — that I was overly impressed by money. "Always have been," he would say. But it wasn't just money; it was the ease and possibilities that money provided, the prospect of a glittering history, and a world that I imagined as lush and green. On Providence Island there were always guests and activities — tennis, golf, sailing, elaborate preparations for a party or for a dance at the Bellisle Club across the channel. At our house there were only old books and greasy playing cards and board games — Scrabble, Monopoly, Clue — jigsaw puzzles with pieces missing, musty old copies of *Country Life*, and Dorothy L. Sayers paperbacks with blotchy yellowing pages.

Over lunch, my aunt and I spoke about the arrangements for the funeral.

"Saint Andrew's United," she said. "You should go out there and talk to the minister."

As far as I knew, my father hadn't been to church in years, not since my mother died.

"But *I* am a member of the church," said Aunt Beth. "And your father used to come with me. From time to time, at any rate."

"He wouldn't have wanted a church service," I said.

"We always have funerals at churches," said Aunt Beth. "It doesn't matter what you believe — funerals are part of a person's spiritual life, the departure of the soul. Birth, marriage, death — all part of the life of the community. The hotel kindly offered to host the reception. They also offered to open some of the rooms early, for visitors from out of town."

"How many are you expecting? Surely there won't be many?"

She frowned. "We'll try to put up as many of the guests as possible at peoples' houses. I think it's so much nicer to stay in someone's home rather than in a hotel, don't you? Especially the Merrick Bay Hotel?"

"Wasn't it a boy from the hotel who helped him back from the lake?"

"It was," said Aunt Beth. "Who knows how long your father would have stood there in the water otherwise? A mystery to me what he was doing. He'd not been behaving oddly lately, nothing like that. Perhaps a little vague sometimes — I put that down to deafness. Eyes like a hawk but couldn't hear a thing. Deafness runs on his mother's side. I suppose you didn't know about that —" she looked at me pointedly "— about your father going deaf, I mean, living — where is it — Idaho? I don't see why a person would want to live in Idaho. Anyway, he was fine earlier that morning. Just fine."

"Could he have been trying to drown himself?"

"In Merrick Bay? At eleven o'clock in the morning? In a foot of water? Anyway, your father wasn't the type."

The truth was that we were both a little afraid that my father might have thought of suicide. No one was the type until they did it. Looking back, I would describe him as melancholic.

"What about the boat?" I asked. "Was it really that old green rowboat from the island?"

"So they say. The boy from the hotel said that your father wanted to set the thing on fire. Why don't you go have a look? They've taken it up to the marina. Philip Havelock wanted to burn the thing, too, but somebody said no. It belongs to the Millers, after all. Besides, the police might want to look at it."

"The police?" It was the boat from which old Mr. Miller fell and drowned more than twenty years before.

"That awful summer," said Aunt Beth. "You remember, the Applewoods … that girl, Marjorie …" She paused, looking at me as though considering whether to say more, then turned and gazed out the window, a plate in each hand. The skin on her arms was like parchment.

"Did Marjorie ever get away to university?" I asked. This brought her out of her trance.

"Does anyone from around here?" said Aunt Beth.

"The brother went to the art college," I said.

But he was a famous exception. In places like Merrick Bay and Iron Falls, the larger town fifteen miles down the highway, school was generally seen in those days as an impediment to the world of work and adulthood, rather than as a means of entry into it. Even the girls, who were brainier, and who were expected to continue in school because there was nothing else for them to do except get into trouble at places like the Rexall Soda Fountain and the Shalomar Tavern, even they were discouraged from any path that might take them too far from the community. The people of Merrick Bay hated airs — people being too big for their britches.

"I remember," Aunt Beth said, "one time at the store hearing Charmaine Ault tell her mother she thought she might like to go away to school, like Marjorie Applewood was planning to. You remember Marjorie wanted to become a high school English teacher, perhaps even a doctor. 'Fine for Marjorie Applewood, but you better learn typing first,' Mrs. Ault said to Charmaine. 'A girl who knows how to type will never be without a job. Bookkeeping, too. We could use some bookkeeping around here.'"

She paused for a moment. "Actually, I think Marjorie did go to teachers' college, somewhere down east."

"You said in your letter the Millers were selling the island," I said. She had also told me that some of the Millers were supposed to be coming up later, after the funeral, I reminded her.

"I suppose that means you'll be staying on, does it?" she asked sharply.

I was not a son of Merrick Bay. The Carriers were outsiders. And although neither were we one of the old families that made up the community at Bellisle, I always liked to see myself as one of the summer people. Aspired, perhaps. I didn't have Aunt Beth's contempt for them.

The next day, despite my protests, my aunt sent me out to St. Andrew's United Church. St. Andrew's-in-the-Fields, my father used to call it: the church was at least four miles back from the lake at crossroads in the middle of hay fields, a place called Merrick Centre. "Centre of what?" I used to ask. Even when I was a boy the other buildings of the hamlet had long since vanished; even the railway through Merrick Station, one concession road to the east, had been torn up.

I remembered driving this road with my parents the first summer we came to Merrick Bay and getting a flat tire in the middle of nowhere. My father couldn't get the bolt off the wheel. The road was low and spongy, just above the muskeg it seemed to me, as though we would gradually sink into the earth if we didn't get out of there, and by dusk no one would be any the wiser. The swamp water was black and I imagined alive with tiny creatures. We stood there in the hot sun, listening to the frogs, the drone of insects, diseased bubbles gurgling up from the swamp. Finally a car came, an ancient black Ford sedan with a sloping trunk. When the man and the boy got out, I saw that the floor of the car was rusted right through; you could see the dirt of the road below. The man said he had a wrench, but he couldn't get the trunk open. So he yanked the back door and told the boy to get in and pull the rear seat forward. The seat wouldn't move. The man started yelling at the boy. "Bust it! Go on! Keep pulling, boy! Bust the goddamn thing!" Finally the seat back gave way with a rip and the boy tumbled out of the car onto the ground. He was about my age. His neck was so dirty it was crosshatched with deep black lines like an old shoe.

When we were on our way again, I asked my parents why those people were dressed like that, about the way they smelled, and what was wrong with them.

"They're just poor," my father said.

I was to meet the minister at two o'clock. My father had been dead five days, the funeral was in three days, the out-of-town people were starting to arrive, and yet arrangements were still being made. In Merrick Bay, as in many small towns, funerals were not even held in the winter; the bodies were stored in a vault at the undertaker's until the ground thawed and the graves could be dug.

We had no family plot, but my aunt was hoping we could put my father out there near the church, anyway. This proved impossible.

"You'll have to get a place at Iron Falls," said the minister. His name was Reverend Hamm. We stood outside because the church would be cold inside — they only fired up the stove on Sundays. And the weather was warm for May, almost like summer, but without the white light or the settled dust everywhere. The fields were the luminous summer yellow-green of my dreams.

"The graveyard here has been closed for sixty years," the minister said, pointing. "Filled with pioneers. Have a look if you like. Not the actual graves of course, everything's been moved around."

The tombstones, about fifty of them altogether, had been assembled into ragged rows inside a rusty fence. I saw the names: Reed, Merrick, Havelock, Alpenvord, Dixon, Macdonald, Mackenzie, MacNab. Some of the oldest stones were the graves of children.

"Do you remember some story — something they found in the swamp?" I asked.

"The swamp? When?"

"Twenty, twenty-five years ago maybe." For some reason, I pretended to be vague.

"Before my time, I'm afraid. Only came up here up ten years ago. I'm from the east, you see," said Reverend Hamm. "Nova Scotia."

We went over the order of service, the readings, some possible hymns, and then he was off; he was responsible for three of these country churches now, he said — the congregations were all in decline, people dying and moving away, what could you expect — and there was a lot of road to cover, terrible roads at that.

Before leaving, I walked around the church. The mortar between the bricks was pocked with holes, and from the open windows you could smell mildew and dampness, the odour of rotting wood.

Before my mother died, my father used to suggest we attend church once or twice a summer. "For tribal reasons," he would say. "Before Union, (he meant the union of the Methodist and Presbyterian Churches) this building was Presbyterian."

It would seem strange to be sitting in church, warm air wafting across the pews from the open windows, and, outside, the buzz of the cicadas. The minister liked to speak to us of something that he called the power of alternative imagining. Four miles away people with gin and tonics would be lounging on the docks by their boathouses. I loved the smell of suntan lotion.

On the way back from the church to my aunt's house, I passed the Applewoods' farm. The built-up banks of Sucker Creek had collapsed and shallow water covered the fields. The roof of the barn had collapsed, too; the house was grey and sagging and the windows were boarded up. It was from one of those windows that I had first set eyes on Quentin Miller.

The stone pump house still stood, as solid as a gravestone, in a grove of weeping willows by the creek.

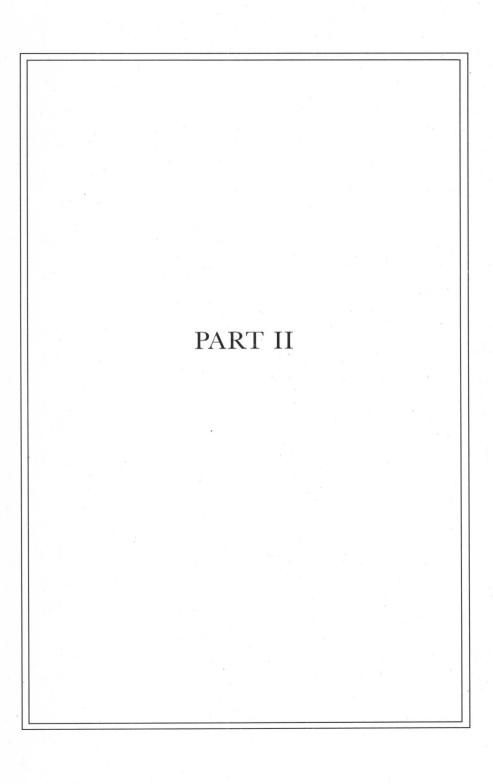

PART II

| CHAPTER 3 |

Late June. In the fading light of dusk, Phil Havelock and I walked through the bush and fields to the Applewoods' farm. Walking wasn't as fast as taking the canoe because you had to skirt the tamarack swamp, but we were in no rush. Besides, it had been a dry winter and spring; the creek was low, and we would have had trouble paddling all the way.

Phil Havelock was almost three years older than me. His family, along with the Applewoods, was one of the last in the area that still farmed. They had a few sheep (at one time the district had been famous for its lamb), chickens, some cattle, and several fields of hay. It was a relative of theirs from whom my father had bought our house. The Havelocks had mixed feelings about my father, partly because the land had been sold out of the family, and partly because they would have liked to sell their own place. All the descendants of the original settlers who had shoreline — the last of the land grants were made as late as the 1890s — had been steadily selling off to summer people, but it was almost impossible to sell land that was back from the lake, pockets of arable interspersed with granite outcrops and swamp. Finding my father had been something of a coup.

Phil and I often caught frogs and crabs for bait and fished in Sucker Creek. "Why don't you go fishing?" my father used to ask. "Boys like fishing, don't they?" He never accompanied me. He swam poorly.

"How come your dad don't swim?" Phil asked me. "He fuckin' English or something? What happens if he falls out of the canoe?"

To my knowledge my father had never once ventured out in the yellow canoe.

When we were younger, Phil and I would build rafts and pole our way up the creek past the Applewoods' farm and as far as the haunted house, the old Allen place, looking for bait. We would hunt for snakes in the pipes and cavities of the Applewoods' pump house — there were supposed to have been huge squirming nests of them there years before, tangled balls — but we never found any. We didn't know then that the snakes were only there from November to June; they migrated to the fields and riverbanks in summer.

Sometimes my aunt let us take the outboard — "Three and a half Jesely horsepower," said Phil, taking a drag on his cigarette. We fished in Merrick Bay, along the inland shore, by some of the islands, or out by the cribs, the ruins of an old steamboat pier that teemed with sunfish, bass, and yellow perch. Or in the haunted lagoon.

In an abandoned drive shed in the corner of the farm property, Phil had amassed a collection of magazines: *Popular Mechanics*, car magazines, and what he called "nudie" magazines. Earlier that afternoon, while we flipped through these for the hundredth time, sharing one of his father's beers and smoking his father's cigarettes, Phil took out his wallet and showed me his condoms. This time he opened one of them. The skin of a long, white worm.

"You put this thing on your dick so she won't have a baby, see?"

What did I care about babies?

"Know what else you can do with them? Make party favours." He began blowing it up. I examined the package. "Take one," said Phil. "I got millions."

"I haven't needed one lately," I said. The foil package was wrinkled and bent. It looked about twenty years old. I didn't believe he had millions.

"You ought to try it with a piece of liver," Phil said. "Feels like the real thing."

"How do you know what the real thing feels like?" I asked.

He smirked. "I know, believe me."

Life in Merrick Bay always seemed to me to be more about birth and death than did life in the city. In the city I was cocooned, insulated; in Merrick Bay I saw things I could never have imagined. Phil and I watched through a slit in the barn door as his father slaughtered a calf. He held an axe, concealed behind his back, as he patted the calf on the head. Then, a lightning-like flash of sunlight on the blade, and he brought the axe around and over his shoulder in an arc and hit the animal on the head with the flat end. The calf bucked forward on its knees and collapsed. Mr. Havelock took a knife from his pocket and slit its throat. He tied a rope to the calf's left rear leg, threw it over a beam, and hauled the carcass up to let the blood drain out. Afterward, in the compost pile, Phil stabbed through a garbage bag to the glistening mass of innards with a pitchfork. These images later became associated in my mind with other things.

I remembered the day the year before when Mr. Applewood died. Mrs. Havelock stood at the back door of the farmhouse, both hands to her face. The people of Merrick Bay thought of Mrs. Havelock as a sweet woman married to a stick. She was involved in the Women's Institute and was often away at meetings or visiting the sick and infirm, and when she was home, she never stopped talking. Mr. Havelock said little. He was a secret drinker: he kept a twenty-four of Dow in the basement and a fifth of Crown Royal in the garage. He would lurk in the yard with a broom with which he chased away the chickens while Mrs. Havelock prattled on. But on that day she was, for once, silent.

Mr. Havelock and Donny, the Applewoods' silent foster son, ran toward the pickup. They had ropes, crowbars, and the chain saw. Phil stood beside the truck.

Mr. Havelock turned and yelled at him: "No, absolutely not. You stay here. Show the ambulance the way when it comes up the road."

The pickup roared away, leaving a cloud of dust settling over the pale grass of the farmyard. Phil and I stood still until the truck was out of sight. Then we ran back toward Sucker Creek. We shoved the yellow canoe into the water and paddled upstream as fast as we could.

"What happened?" I asked Phil. "What's going on?"

"You'll see."

After we passed through the tamarack swamp, the creek broadened to a wide bend and the land suddenly seemed to open up — a clearing in the forest like a secret garden. The Applewoods' farm was out of place there: neat fields, a perfect green barn, and, on a small hill in the distance, a white frame house with green trim. By a stand of poplars, between the creek and the field closest to the old pump house, we saw a group of figures. We saw the Havelocks' pickup and other cars driving across the fields. As we drew closer, I spotted a tractor overturned in the grass near the trees, one of those oddly thin Massey-Fergusons with the front wheels close together, the kind of tractor people used to scythe grass or plough vegetable gardens. And then the immense roots of a poplar tree that had toppled over, pulling itself loose from the spongy bank of the creek. We scrambled ashore. Through the leaves I saw a hand, palm to the sky although the man lay on his stomach. The hand was faintly blue. The man's eyes, half-open, were still bright. The trunk of the tree had missed him, but a large branch lay across his back. The branch looked as though it were just resting on Mr. Applewood, that he might stand up and brush it aside. It had crushed him to death.

The buzz of a chain saw. In the distance I saw Mrs. Applewood with her arms around the neck of a girl. Marjorie Applewood. She had dark hair and large dark eyes that shone with tears.

Now, with Mr. Applewood gone, the farm was beginning to slip. The front gate was off its hinges and the lawn at the side of the driveway was going to seed with dandelions and plantain. There was a harrow with grass growing through the tines and a couple of old cars up on blocks — a common sight along the back roads of the district, but incongruous in front of the Applewoods' still bright green barn.

The cars were Donny's: junkers that he brought home and sold in bits and pieces to garages and body shops. When Mr. Applewood was alive, Donny had to keep the cars out behind the barn. Donny was the Applewoods' foster child, had lived with them since he was four years old. Some people said he wasn't quite right in the head. I thought he was just quiet. Scary quiet.

But Phil Havelock seemed to understand Donny, and he knew people like Chicklet, too, who lived in the district year-round and attended the high school at Iron Falls, and the big Indian from Parry Sound that everyone called Spook. Phil and his friends went to bars — the Shalomar, just beyond the village, or the Golden Dragon, down the highway. Phil was almost nineteen, but he looked about twenty-five. He was six feet tall and had a dark beard. He was starting to go bald. He had deep wings and a bare spot on the back of his head the size of a silver dollar, and the beginnings of a paunch. Phil was working around the farm that summer and helping his father look after the summer places. In September he would even have to pay rent, which I thought was very strange. The good news was he had his driver's licence.

We'd been sitting in the Havelocks' kitchen, listening to Phil's mother talk. She talked endlessly about the families in the district and what they were doing: the MacNabs, the Aults, the Reeds, the Merricks, what was left of them. And the Applewoods, especially the Applewoods, poor Marjorie and Donny — not quite right in the head, if you asked her — and now the father dead and all, and the mother starting to go just a little funny, too, and the older brother gone to study art in Toronto.

"Art school. Can you imagine? Someone from Merrick Bay, an *artist*?" she said. "Although I'm not surprised, really. The mother has brains. And look at the job his father did on the barn, God rest his soul. But how can they afford it — that's the question I ask myself."

And then she'd mentioned the party.

"What?" said Phil.

"A party," said his mother, "at Marjorie Applewood's. Supper, next Thursday. It's going to be a barbecue. Hot dogs. All the Coke you can drink!"

"Shit," said Phil, rolling his eyes. "Miss Goody-Goody has a fucking tea party."

"Philip Havelock!"

"Pardon my French, Mother. I'll wash my mouth with soap."

The reason for the party was that the Applewoods had rented out the farmhouse and would soon be moving into another smaller place nearby, and to mark the finish of the school year for Marjorie and her friends. In the end, Phil had agreed to go and had dragged me along.

When we arrived and I introduced myself, Marjorie blurted, "I know who *you* are. *You're* Ray Carrier. Your father brought the old river house from Phil Havelock's uncle. I met you at the Havelocks' place when I came to deliver honey, last summer, and once at Ault's store. I work there mornings, helping out Charmaine. You were there with your aunt, carrying boxes out to the car." She spoke these words all in a rush. Then she paused and touched my wrist. She turned toward the barbecue. "Here, help me light this stupid thing. It keeps going out."

It was a small party. Besides myself, Phil Havelock, and Marjorie and Donny Applewood, there were Chicklet and his sister, who lived on a farm down the road; Henri LaTroppe, who lived in a room above the Shell station in Merrick Bay and had arrived at the party on a motorcycle; Monica and Clarrisa, two giggling girls from Marjorie's high school in Iron Falls; and Charmaine Ault from Merrick Bay, whose mother owned the general store. Chicklet used to say, "Know what? Charmaine Ault?" He would make a pumping gesture with his right hand and provide sound effects by working the chewing gum in his mouth. He always had gum in his mouth, his name was Jerry Reed, and everyone called him Chicklet. He had bright darting eyes and a brush cut. "Yeah, you try to touch her hooters, she thinks it's real bad, like the devil's going to get her? So she rubs it for you just to keep your hands off of her." He would speak in a breathy voice — "Oh, Ray, it's so *big*. Oh, Ray, let me look after it for you. Let me *stroke* it. Here, Ray, hold *these*," — and stick out his chest to imitate Marilyn Monroe.

Chicklet and Phil and I used to horse around in the stream where it pooled beside the old hen house at the back of our garden. The creek bed was red clay; you could duck-dive underwater and grab handfuls of it, make ashtrays, paperweights, and little bowls. One time Chicklet made a figurine, with great round breasts, long nipples, and an enormous penis. He placed it, temple-like, on the back of the bird feeder.

"What is it?" I asked.

"A fertility god. Someone around here's going to get pregnant. Maybe

Aunt Beth." He began a fertility dance around the bird feeder.

An upstairs sash clattered open. Aunt Beth called out: "Jerry Reed, what on *earth* are you doing?"

"Keeping the cougars away," said Jerry.

"There aren't any cougars around here," said Aunt Beth.

"It's working!" said Jerry.

Donny Applewood (several years older than even Phil and Henri LaTroppe) lurked in the background sucking a beer. He wore dirty jeans, black boots, and a black T-shirt with a package of Export "A"s tucked in the sleeve. He was pasty-faced, and so thin his chest was concave — six feet tall, but he couldn't have weighed more than a hundred and forty. He had greasy hair, a wispy goatee, and acne. He'd once thrown a brick at Mr. Applewood, cut him for seven stitches. He used to mark his place in the dirty books he read with old razor blades so the teachers at the high school would cut their fingers when they tried to snatch them away from his shirt pocket. As I passed to get more kindling, he raised his bottle and said in a low voice, "Beer?" He never addressed anyone by name.

After the hot dogs, Marjorie put some music on and tried to get people to dance on the porch. She came down the wooden steps to where Phil, Chicklet, and I skulked in the shadows. She took Chicklet and me by the hands and led us to the porch. Chicklet was to dance with Monica. He turned to me and rolled his eyes.

The record that Marjorie had put on was a slow one, and she sang softly along with the words. Her breath was hot in my ear.

> Why does the sun go on shining?
> Why does the sea rush to shore?
> Don't they know it's the end of the world,
> 'Cause you don't love me anymore.

Marjorie leaned in and put her hot hands on my neck. I could feel the curves and hollows of her body. She smelled of lilac-sweet perfume and sweet perspiration.

"What *does* it mean, Ray?" she asked, turning her face up to mine. "Why *does* the sun go on shining?"

"Christ, I don't know," I said.

Footsteps behind us: Donny had left Phil and Henri LaTroppe out by the barn to guard the case of beer. He crossed over to the swing couch where the other two girls were sitting.

"Want to dance?" he asked Charmaine Ault.

"No, thanks," said Charmaine.

"Oh, come on, Char," said Marjorie. "It's a party. Dance with my brother. He doesn't bite."

"That's not what I heard," said Charmaine. She stood up and rolled her eyes, "Oh, all *right*."

Marjorie Applewood whispered in my ear, "I write poetry."

"What about?"

"About your mother. You know. Dying."

"My mother?"

"About airplanes crashing and horrible fires in the woods, houses burning down, people drowning. Death. About my father, I write about that, too. And, of course, love."

She took me by the hand and led me upstairs to her room. We sat on the bed. She unlocked the drawer in the side table and took out a black school scribbler. Her arm touched mine as we sat on the bed and she showed me the neatly printed pages. I was finding it difficult to concentrate on the poetry — the beer, the warmth radiating from Marjorie Applewood's skin, the down on her arms. The short skirt that had ridden up her thigh. The bed. My erection.

"Do you miss your mother?" she asked.

"Sometimes, I guess."

"You're not like the people around here. You know that, Ray, don't you?"

We leaned toward each other. The walls of the room were blue. Her lips were red. I felt the brush of her tongue.

But then through the calico curtains — hazy headlights: an automobile fast up the drive. I heard the sound of spitting gravel. The car lurched to a stop on the lawn, beneath a dim light high on a telephone pole. A maroon Buick station wagon. The sound from the car radio drowned out the record player on the porch.

"Who's that?" one of the girls downstairs asked. Marjorie raced down the stairs, leaving me holding the scribbler.

Three people piled out of the back seat of the car: two boys and a girl. One of the boys was fat. They were tanned. They wore pastel Bermuda shorts, button-down shirts, and loafers without socks. They were drunk and laughing, waving their beers around.

"Get back in that car and move it." Marjorie stood by the open passenger side door, hands on her hips. "Who do you think you are? You can't just drive up and park on the grass. And turn that radio down!"

"I thought this was a party," said the fat boy. He leaned against the car, grinning stupidly.

But someone did turn the car radio down. From the window of Marjorie's bedroom, I saw that two people were still in the car, the driver and a woman beside him. I couldn't see her features, but she had her arms folded across her chest and she didn't look relaxed. The driver opened his door and put one foot out, but he remained seated, smoking a cigarette.

"Turn out those headlights!" someone yelled from the porch.

"So, it's a party. Who invited you?" Marjorie said. "And on top of everything else, your friend is being sick."

Sure enough, behind the station wagon, the other boy (Radley Smith, I would learn was his name) was bent over, throwing up in the petunias. The girl who had got out of the car went to tend him, although she kept her distance. The faces of the two who remained in the car were shrouded in darkness.

Phil and Charmaine came out of the shadows and into the light cast by the lamp on the telephone pole.

"It's Jethro and Ellie May!" said the fat boy, laughing again. He drained the rest of what looked like a Budweiser — the long-necked bottle was exotic — and threw it into the darkness behind him.

"Watch your fuckin' mouth, fat boy," said Phil.

From the porch, Chicklet yelled, "Turn out those headlights! We can't see a damn thing up here."

"All right, you go out there, right now, and pick up that bottle," said Marjorie, pointing to the dark field.

"Oh, yeah, right," said the fat one. "Like I can see in the dark?"

Henri and Donny materialized out of the darkness by the barn. Donny was carrying a crowbar.

"What…?" said the fat one, standing up straight. Even the boy who had been vomiting stood, watching Donny.

Henri stopped at the edge of the circle of light. Donny loped past the front of the car. He raised the crowbar and swung it down hard. The sound of breaking glass shattered the night.

The driver bolted from the car. "Jesus Christ!" He moved toward the front of the car. He was tall and he looked strong, but Donny had the crowbar. "Look," he said, waving his hand at the darkness. "How are we going to see to get out of here?"

"Your fucking problem," said Donny. He raised the crowbar to smash out the other light, but the woman in the car reached across to the driver's side and switched it off. That was when I saw her.

Donny lowered the crowbar and faded into the darkness. The girl in the car shifted over to the driver's seat, started the engine, and backed carefully off the lawn. She leaned toward the open passenger door. "Come on, Jack. Let's get out of here."

While the fat boy and Radley Smith scrambled back into the car, the tall boy came forward into the pool of yellow light where Marjorie still stood. He looked down at the scars the tires had gouged into the lawn, the broken glass from the headlight.

"Sorry about the grass," he said. "I guess the broken light means we're even." He held out his hand and smiled at Marjorie, a toothy grin. "I'm Jack Miller. You must be Marjorie. We really *were* invited to your party, you know. My sister and I." He gestured toward the car. "We're out at Providence Island. Your mother —"

He stopped mid-sentence. I suppose he didn't want to sound condescending. After the death of her husband, Mrs. Applewood had started doing a little work for some of the summer people, including the Millers. She had asked Mrs. Miller if Jack and Quentin would like to come to her daughter's party. Mrs. Miller would have wondered how she could say no.

I had met Jack's brother Stephen once when he chased Phil and me when I was about thirteen. We used to throw milkweeds in clumps of earth at passing cars from the bluffs above the highway. Sometimes a car would stop, and we would run into the woods. One time a man in a convertible — he would have been about eighteen years old then — screeched on the brakes, jumped from the car without opening the doors, and ran up the bank. Phil headed for the underbrush, while I ran across an open field. I heard the man panting behind me — then he leaped through the air and caught me by the foot; he grabbed me by the shoulder, turned me over. He was about to hit me, but when he saw the split in my lip from the fall, he held back.

"What's your name?" He was red in the face and panting. "The police will be by your house later."

"No appetite?" asked my father at dinner that night.

"What have you been up to?" Aunt Beth asked. "How did you get that cut lip?"

The police never came. The next day in Phil's cellar we smoked a couple of his father's Export "A"s and split one of his beers.

"You know who that guy in the fuckin' convertible was?" asked Phil. "One of those Miller assholes."

"Who are they?"

"Who are they? They only own pretty near the biggest fuckin' place in the islands. That's who."

That had been my first meeting with the Millers. The man in the convertible was Stephen Miller, Jack's older brother. Seven years later he was killed in Vietnam, near the Cambodian border.

There was a squeaking in the ceiling above us. Phil's father was home, back from one of the summer cottages he looked after. We heard him stop dead in the middle of the room. Sniffing the air, Phil motioned me not to speak. We carefully buried our cigarettes in the dirt of the basement floor and rolled the empty beer bottle along the pipes under the water heater.

The kitchen door opened, throwing a beam of light down the wooden stairs.

"Boy, you down there? Jesus Christ, answer me!"

Mr. Havelock started clumping down the stairs. He was a gnarly little man with red hair. Years of work on the farm and then at the gravel pit had given him a stoop, but he could move quickly. He held his broom above his head like a sabre. As soon as I saw his feet on the stairs, I ran for the ladder that led to the cellar door and the yard. I heard him as I left: "Goddamn it, boy, I told you to stay out of my beer," and the sound of the broom as he swiped at Phil.

"I'm sorry," Jack said to Marjorie. "Sorry we're late. I shouldn't have brought my friends along. I thought it would be a bigger party." He looked toward the house, to the little group standing around the porch steps and on the lawn, the boys clutching their stubby brown beer bottles.

"Come on, Jack," said the girl. "Let's go."

Because of the run-in with his brother, I had known about Jack and the Millers, known about Providence Island — that it was there, like the other summer places — but it had had nothing to do with me. Now I'd seen them: drunk and tanned, carelessly dressed in their expensive clothes. They were around my age. Hard to believe. Jack was supposed to be some kind of schoolboy hockey star, headed for Harvard or Cornell.

What they must have seen, I couldn't help thinking — hated myself for seeing it, too: the gate off its hinges, the overgrown drive, Donny's wrecks up on blocks in front of the barn. As they neared the house, they would have seen a few people dancing to a tinny record player on the porch, mosquitoes and moths fluttering around the yellow bulbs. Donny, Phil, Henri, and Jerry Reed in their jeans and T-shirts. Charmaine Ault: perhaps they would have recognized her from the store where some of the people from the islands and the summer places had accounts. Charmaine and her famous sloppy tits. And Monica and Clarrisa, hiding in the shadows, giggling. Watching.

Marjorie Applewood didn't hide. She stood on the lawn watching the red tail lights vanish into the night.

I watched, too — hidden in the upstairs window.

| CHAPTER 4 |

Marjorie came up the stairs. She snatched the scribbler from my hands and locked it away in the drawer. She had lost interest in me, in the party, in her poems. She was annoyed, not because the Millers had come, but because they hadn't come — and because her mother hadn't told her that she had invited them.

A few days later, Phil showed me the dark green clapboard garage behind the Merrick Bay Hotel. "This place belongs to Providence Island," he said.

We peeked through the windows. The 1942 Packard limousine and an old Morgan sports car were kept at Merrick Bay year-round. There was also a late model Cadillac and a station wagon. These cars were put away at the beginning of the summer, after the Millers arrived; the ones they used every day, including the maroon Buick that we had seen at the party, were kept at the Bellisle Club.

Back home, I was ashamed of our house: it wasn't on the lake nor was it a summer house. It was a farm that had stood ramshackle and abandoned until my father bought it. I felt he had been duped.

I rode my bike out to the highway, past the village of Merrick Bay, and down the dirt road to the landing at Bellisle. I watched the mahogany launches cruise in from the islands. Boxes of groceries from Ault's or Merrick's Butchers were loaded into the boats. And liquor, cases of it. I loved the throaty roar the launches made as they sped away from the pier. In the parking lot were big sedans and station wagons from Pennsylvania, Michigan, and New York State. From the landing you could see some of the boathouses, but most of the big places were out of sight, beyond the pine headlands and the open waters of the bay.

I would see them arrive for the sailboat races, or with their tennis racquets and golf clubs. The boys wore Bass Weejuns, faded madras shirts, and Bermuda shorts of pale cotton. The girls — long-limbed, tanned, and clear-skinned — wore polo shirts or men's oxford shirts and sweater-coats from prep schools whose names I didn't know. Downy blond hair on their arms.

I mentioned at dinner that I thought I might take up golf.

My aunt snorted. "What you need is a summer job. I'll ask around."

It did not take her long. Mrs. Applewood, for whom my father had done a little legal work around the time of her husband's death, telephoned a week later. She was working on Providence Island, helping the French-Canadian girls in the kitchen (she was an excellent cook, famous in Merrick Bay for her church suppers) and looking after old J.D. Miller, who had suffered a stroke and needed help making his way around the island. The Millers were celebrating seventy-five years on Providence Island and there was to be a big party. Mrs. Applewood said they were looking for extra staff.

She told me more about the place; I had the impression that Mrs. Applewood knew quite a lot about Providence Island. Behind the latticework and screening of one of the side verandahs of the big house, she told me, there was a games room for rainy days (Ping-Pong, billiards, darts), a barbershop, and laundry facilities big enough to serve a small hotel. The houses on the mainland that the Millers used to provide for the chauffeur and the butler were larger than the houses most people lived in year-round. There had at one time been a housekeeper, a cook, an assistant cook, two maids, a full-time gardener, a garden helper, and two men to polish and tend to the fleet of boats.

Now the only people who worked there were a couple of shy girls from rural Quebec, a gardener-handyman, a couple of boys from the village who worked around the boathouses in return just for being near the boats, and Mrs. Applewood.

And now, seventy-five years later, Mrs. Applewood and others still sometimes talked of how it used to be: parties under the stars, the long mahogany launches, thin women in diaphanous dresses, romance, the sheen of money. I was enchanted, but not my father.

"You know how they make their money, don't you?" he said. "They own warehouses, and these shopping place things — what d'you call them? — *plazas*."

From the way he spoke, it was hard to imagine anything more vile.

"Before that they were in liquor," said Aunt Beth. She was a teetotaller.

"They don't want people around here to sell their land because it might spoil the view from their docks," said my father. Some of the people who wanted to sell were clients of his. "Yet they made their own money in real estate," he said. "They use the money down there —" he meant the cities where they lived year-round "— to buy politicians. Greasing palms. Up here they try to prevent plain people from selling their land."

My father liked the idea of living in a place where the farmers were descendants of the original settlers — he had shown me old titles, land grants from Queen Victoria — and he hated the Bellisle Club. He had been to boarding school as a boy, an experience he loathed, and had been affected by the son of one of the schoolmasters who fell in with rich boys. "Ruined his life. He couldn't understand where it came from, all that money, and why he couldn't have it. Ended up in jail."

"I won't end up in jail," I said.

"Don't be a smarty pants," said Aunt Beth. "Perhaps we could find you something else to do. Something more suitable."

"I've already taken the job," I said.

"I predict disaster," said my father. "Pass the salt."

Jack Miller met us at the Bellisle landing the day before the party. He was wearing white trousers and a straw hat and was accompanied by a lame

Irish setter called Beau. The dog smelled.

There were six of us who had been hired to help out at the anniversary party. I noticed that I was the only one from the summer community; the others were all local people from Merrick Bay.

Jack asked us our names.

"Carrier?" he asked, as if it were perhaps a local name he ought to recognize. "Where do you live?"

"The old river road," I mumbled. We lived on a county road that didn't have a proper name.

"Don't know it," he said.

We crossed the channel in Jack's inboard. I had seen boats like it, but never actually been in one. The seats were red leather. The fittings were polished to a high sheen. I was familiar, too, with what they called the back of Providence Island from fishing the black waters there in our little outboard, but I had never been to the south end, where the buildings were, and where we were now headed.

Every June the Millers, relatives, and friends, began gathering for their summer on Providence Island. The house had cedar shingle-clad towers, and wide verandahs with wicker furniture. There were supposed to be twenty-seven bedrooms, including those for the staff. In the attic there was a doll's house that was larger than the one owned by the royal family, pictures of which had been in the weekend *Star* colour supplement. Beneath the water tower, on a flat hill high in the middle of the island, there was supposed to be a cache of liquor, hidden there by the Millers during Prohibition. I wondered what kind of homes there were in New York, Philadelphia, Pittsburgh, Palm Beach, and the other places where the Millers lived the rest of the year.

The ones nearest my age were Jack and Quentin. I came to think of them as brother and sister, as I discovered they did themselves, but the relationship was actually more complicated: Jack's grandfather, J.D., was Quentin's father; she was the product of a short marriage to an actress in a film that he had financed. (These complicated marital arrangements were the sort of thing to which my father would never allude.) The actress — long-gone by the time I knew the Millers, bought off, it was said, to avoid newspaper stories — remained famous locally for having exposed her breasts on Regatta Day. Quentin was raised by Jack's mother.

As we approached, I saw the glint of more mahogany and chrome through the boathouse doors. We docked at the largest boathouse, which had four slips and a long pier. Workmen were attaching additional floating docks for the party. A couple of us would be here throughout the evening, Jack explained, helping people dock and moving boats when the guests were leaving.

Jack led us along the broad gravel paths through the lawns and woods, which had been groomed to allow views of the water. We passed a red clay tennis court, other boathouses, and swimming docks (we weren't to park boats there in case people wanted to bathe during the party). We went upstairs to an immense room with balconies cantilevered over the water. The dance pavilion, Jack called it.

At the tip of the island, an expansive T-shaped dock gave long views to the south and west. The flags on the mast snapped in the wind. This is where we would deliver the guests who were arriving by car at the Bellisle Club.

"Which of you is going to help up at the house?"

Nobody answered.

"Ray, is it? Come with me."

A gravel walk led up to the house, through a lawn groomed like a golf green. A dance floor had been set up on the lawn, as well, and workmen were putting up a blue-striped canopy and strings of coloured lights. A small orchestra would play there for the older generation.

Jack led me through the front hall and living room, smelling of old wood and leather, to the verandah, dazzling white with sunlight. Mrs. Miller and Quentin — I recognized her at once — both wore tennis clothes. Quentin's hair was tied loosely with a bandana. She was slim, eighteen, and to me she looked like a movie star — somehow familiar. Mrs. Miller sat in a white wicker armchair. Her gold hair was pulled back in a chignon. Quentin leaned against one of the pillars, her arm languid atop the letter *M* ensconced in the patterned diamonds of the verandah railing. Between them was a glass table piled with magazines and an oversize ashtray, blue smoke curling up. A white drinks trolley was at the ready with chunky glasses and bottles of vermouth, gin, rum, and vodka.

Jack said, "This is where the main bar will be." Then he introduced me.

"Ray Carrier?" asked Mrs. Miller. "Is your father the lawyer who bought the old farmhouse on Sucker Creek?"

I nodded.

"Heavens, shouldn't you be *coming* to the party, not picking up the dirty glasses?"

I mumbled something about being glad to have the work, but it had been a rhetorical question. She ran a hand through her hair, turned away, took a sip of her gin and tonic.

Quentin leaned against the column, watching. She seemed flushed; her lips were dry. She must have just finished playing tennis. She nodded when we were introduced. Nothing more.

Jack said, "I'll show you the kitchen."

When I told them at home about my visit to Providence Island, my aunt changed her mind about the job. "They want you to wear dark pants and a white shirt? Do they think you are one of the servants? I would tell them to pick up their own glasses, if I were you. Talk to the municipality. You could get a job helping tar the roads. I know they take on summer help. Surely that would be better than serving hard liquor to silly people."

But it was too late. I was listening to my aunt, but I was thinking about Quentin Miller, leaning against the porch post. Her tanned legs.

The evening of the party I circulated through the rooms of the big house, picking up glasses. Voices and laughter, music from the orchestra, and the thudding base from the pavilion filled the evening air. Caterers who had come up from the city carried drinks on silver trays and served cold salmon, lobster, and pink beef tenderloin from behind tables draped with linen. The waiters wore stiff white jackets and called everyone sir or madam.

Several of the guests arrived by seaplane. One group came from New York City in a private jet that landed at the airport at Iron Falls. The Millers provided a car and driver to pick them up.

"Where did all the money come from, anyway?" I heard someone ask.

"Liquor."

"But this place was built years before Prohibition."

"Railroads," said someone else.

"Real estate," said another. "They're nothing but developers."

"The old man was in movies," said a woman of about thirty-five in a gauzy see-through blue top. "You remember — his second wife was it — an actress? He brought her up here once, years ago."

"Did he actually marry her?" asked the other.

At seven thirty, two hours after most of the guests had arrived, Jack appeared in the pantry. He said, "You play tennis, don't you?"

I nodded.

"We need a fourth. I'll lend you some shoes, a pair of shorts."

"What about the dirty glasses?"

"Forget the glasses."

He led me to a wing of the house with several bedrooms and bathrooms and with a separate dressing room with floor-to-ceiling shelves and drawers. This was where he and his brothers Stephen and Robert stayed, along with various visiting friends and male cousins. He opened a wardrobe; one cedar shelf was filled with laundered tennis shirts, another with perhaps twenty pairs of shorts.

"You pick something. There are running shoes in the cupboard. I'll see you on the court."

Quentin, Jack, and the person called Radley Smith were hitting the ball when I arrived. We played for an hour, finishing under the lights. Afterward, we sat by the dock. There was a Coca-Cola cooler, like in a store, just inside the door of the boathouse, and we helped ourselves.

"Where did you learn to play?" Quentin asked. These were the first words she addressed to me.

"At school. They're big on hockey and football. If you're no good, they ship you off to the community tennis club."

"Hmm," she turned away, gazing out toward the water and the orange sky to the west.

"You don't play hockey?" asked Jack. "Or football?"

"I guess I'm too refined," I said. No one laughed. The conversation turned to other matters.

"Where's your date, Jack?" Radley Smith asked.

"He doesn't have one," said Quentin. "Jack's got his eye on some farm girl he met in Merrick Bay."

"Local talent," said Radley Smith. "When do we meet her?"

"Never, if I can help it," said Jack.

"You sneaking off again tonight?" asked Quentin.

"Really, what's she like?" asked Smith.

Jack shrugged.

"Maybe Ray knows her," said Quentin. "Maybe he can tell you all about her, Radley."

Quentin strolled to the end of the dock, stripped off her tennis clothes, and dived into the lake. It was dusk, but I saw her skin flash against the water, and I saw the pale hollows of her body. By the time we followed her into the water, she had headed up to the house in a towel to change. I didn't see her again until the end of the evening when I was ferrying my last load of guests back to the mainland. She had changed into a white sleeveless sundress. She was supervising the guest book, set up on the dock on a kind of lectern. When the people I was to drive across the channel finished signing, she held out the pen to me. "You might as well sign. You played tennis with us."

| CHAPTER 5 |

In the days following I was invited to Providence Island often, to make up a fourth for tennis or complete a round robin. They would phone and ask me to be there at two o'clock, occasionally in the morning, and to always wear whites; that was a rule I broke only once — they wouldn't let me on the court. Someone would be sent to pick me up from the government wharf at Merrick Bay, or I would chug over in our little outboard. A couple of times I arrived to find that there had been a change in plans; they had gone golfing or sailing, and I would return home half an hour later.

"Are you at their beck and call?" Aunt Beth would ask.

The answer to which was yes. I was glad to be away from our house: the click of my aunt's knitting needles as she studied the crossword puzzles, her tea and bridge; my father, when he was there, reading, fiddling with the radio and railing on about the government. There was none of that kind of talk at the Millers. There was very little serious talk at all on Providence Island, mostly plans for activities and meals and who was coming and going, gossip about the members of the Bellisle Club. Everybody seemed to be having affairs.

One morning Jack took me on a boat tour of the grand houses of Bellisle. "Millionaires' Row," it was of course called. He stopped in front of one of the few newer places, a sprawling palace of glass and steel. A blond woman in a short terry-cloth robe appeared on the front terrace. She waved at us. "My father's having an affair with her," Jack said.

They were always listening to Frank Sinatra records. (I asked my father about this: "Do all your generation like Frank Sinatra?" "No," he answered. "The man's some kind of racketeer, isn't he?") They never talked about politics. Old J.D. Miller had been in the U.S. Senate and Jack's father was already preparing to run for Congress. One day Jack would run for office.

I explained this to my father. "The Millers never talk about politics," I said. "They don't have to. They're *in* politics."

My father put down his book and stared at me. On the radio they were in the final act of *La Bohème*. "I see," he said.

The Millers started asking me to stay — for a swim, for a glass of lemonade, sometimes for lunch. I would occasionally see Mrs. Applewood, bringing food out from the pantry or guiding old J.D. up and down the path to the dock, or on his afternoon walk around the island. He was strong, but the paths through the woods were up-and-down, rocky, and ungroomed, and he needed help there. He used a single black cane. With his other hand he held on to Mrs. Applewood, either by her shoulder or by the arm just above her elbow. Mrs. Applewood nodded to me when she passed, as though she hardly knew me, meaning to avoid embarrassing us both, I suppose. J.D.'s gnarled grip was a large claw on her arm.

One July afternoon, when the sun was high and the tennis balls fell lifeless on the baked red clay of the court, Jack, Radley, and I decided that we would go for a swim while we waited for the court and the day to cool down enough to play.

On the way to the boathouse to change, Jack took me aside. "Do you know this girl, Marjorie Applewood?"

I nodded. "I know who you mean," I said, distancing myself.

"I met her at the start of the summer," Jack continued. "Some god-awful party in the boonies. Her mother works here, you know, and she set it up with my mother. Big mistake, I guess. Anyway, I've been out there a few times to see her. You know — these farm girls." He winked. "Now she won't talk to me. I haven't seen her in over a week. Maybe you can find out something about it. You know these people? That French guy who pumps gas at the Shell station, and his buddy Havelock, the bald guy? They're friends of Marjorie's. Maybe you could ask them, see if she's gone away somewhere?"

For some reason I wasn't very keen on asking around about Marjorie on Jack's behalf.

"You could go to Ault's store," I said. "Marjorie works there most mornings."

"I've tried that. Apparently she's quit."

"Why don't you just ask her mother? She's out here nearly every day, isn't she?"

"I would, but the thing is, she doesn't know about Marjorie and me. It's kind of a secret." He stared at me. "So, are you going to do it? Find out what's going on for me?"

"If it's such a secret, I better ask Marjorie myself."

"Great." He slapped me on the shoulder.

Suddenly I needed a break from the Millers. I changed my mind and declined the offer of a swim with Jack and Radley. "I think I'll walk up to the tower. See if I can't find that liquor that's supposed to hidden up there."

"Watch yourself around that tower. Thing's rotting through," Jack said.

On the flat, high hill in the middle of the island there were a couple of small ponds from which in spring freshets flowed through the woods and stony gullies to the lake. In summer the runnels were dry and fringed by ferns, like ruins of ancient steps carved from stone. It was hard work climbing the hill. The footing was unsteady. Near the top I disturbed a bird, a grouse perhaps, which shot up with a clatter.

It was hard to tell where the cache of liquor might be, near what stump, what pile of stone. If it ever really was there. Unlikely, anyway, that the bottles could have survived these long winters. I gave up and headed toward a plateau, and the woods opened up, a glade with oaks and maple and white pine. The ground became soft and damp, and the smell of the earth was rich, almost rotten. There were several ways to turn. I heard the gurgle of water, then a woman's voice. A sigh, a moan. I turned away, but I had seen them through the maple leaves as through a jalousie, dappled by sun and shadow.

I didn't recognize the man. But there was no doubt about the girl. Her blond hair. Her voice.

| CHAPTER 6 |

What did I actually know about Quentin Miller? That she was rich and thin and languid. She played tennis. She would go to Wellesley College in the fall. She stripped naked in front of people when she wanted to swim, thought nothing of it. Her pubic hair was blond. What I had seen — not seen — flickering through the leaves … it burned in my brain like a hallucination.

I was determined to know more. Getting to know Jack better, that would be the key. (This seemed natural to me, not at all devious.) And what Jack wanted was to find out something about Marjorie Applewood. Marjorie Applewood was sixteen years old, a farm girl, and, I thought, a bit moony since her father had died. I remembered the small bedroom where she had shown me her poetry, the bedspread pink and frilly, the stuffed animals on the bookshelf, the faint smell of barnyard wafting through the window, the scent of her body laced with sweet lilac perfume.

I asked Phil about her at the Shalomar the next night. He thought I was the one who was interested.

"Marjorie Applewood?" he asked. "There must be some mistake."

"Miss Goody-Goody," said Chicklet. That was what the boys at the high school called her.

"She's just a little girl," said Henri LaTroppe. Henri was supposed to have a girlfriend in Iron Falls. Her name was Dulcy, and she was thirty-two years old. "You need to get some *action*, buddy-boy? Charmaine Ault. Ask her. Ask her to the drive-in at Iron Falls."

"We'll hide in the trunk," said Chicklet, "and whisper, tell you what to do next, where to put it."

Henri signalled for the waiter. The table was covered with peanut shells and empty draft glasses. They had only served me because I had come in with Phil and Henri; Phil looked legal age and Henri *was* legal. Henri also knew the owner — fixed his cars for him — and he was friends with the bouncer, a smooth-faced Ojibway from north of Parry Sound who everyone called Spook. Henri said that he was part Indian himself, that he was descended from coureurs de bois, but nobody believed him. His father worked at the mines in Sudbury.

The Tap Room of the Shalomar smelled like a urinal. There were always a few old men there in the back, smoking and mumbling to themselves. Five bikers were at the table next to us, members of the local chapter of Black Heart Riders. Phil and Henri knew most of them, from the school in Iron Falls.

"Hey, Ray, you're in luck. Look who just came in," Phil said. He nudged me with his elbow and pointed through to the other room. The Shalomar was divided in half, a holdover from the days of the old provincial liquor laws. The Tap Room used to be the men's beverage room; the Starlite Lounge had been for ladies and escorts. The rooms were separated by a couple of oversize double doors that were now always open. From our table in the Tap Room, we could see the bandstand, the snack bar with its jars of brown pickled eggs and pepperoni sticks, and the small dance floor in the Starlite Lounge.

"This is your big chance," said Phil.

Charmaine's purple tank top glowed under the neon beer signs. Phil waved her over. She pretended not to see him. Then I saw why: she was with Jack Miller, Radley Smith, and a couple of others from the Bellisle Club.

"Hey, aren't those your new friends, Ray?" asked Chicklet. "The boys in *madras*?"

I looked down at my beer. I didn't want Jack Miller or Radley Smith to see me here. Perhaps Quentin was with them. Perhaps she would be joining them.

From the next table, one of the bikers said, "Hey, Bert, isn't that your old lady?"

"Eh?" said the one next to him. He wore a sleeveless vest, had pink eyes, acne scars, and a wispy moustache that was fringed with beer foam. You could smell their leather jackets.

"Char Ault. In there." The first biker gestured with his glass toward the Starlite Lounge. "By the door. Sitting with a couple of faggots."

"Fucking *A*," said another biker, a fat pimply one.

"Shit," said the one with pig's eyes and the foamy moustache.

"Nice language," said Phil, loud enough so that they could hear.

"Fuck you. Fuckin' hayseed," said Bert, the pig-eyed one.

"Temper, temper, Bertram," said Phil, scolding with his finger, and speaking like a school marm. "You talk like that, I'm going to have to report you. Demerits."

"Fucking cocksucker. Who you think you're talking to?" Bert half rose from his chair. "And don't call me Bertram, 'less you want your fuckin' legs broken. Fuckin' asshole."

"What we need here," said Henri, eyes glistening, "is a good fight." He leaned forward, reached behind his back into his belt loop, and pulled out a knife. He spun the knife beneath the lip of the table, so that only those at the next table could see it. The blade glittered in the dim light.

Bert faltered and drew back, glancing around the table for support. He hitched up his vest, and I saw that under it he had a knife, too. The roll of his stomach padded the hilt.

Then the largest biker at the other table — he'd been silent so far, smoothing his long moustache and watching — said, "Cool it." The others sat down.

"Fuck," said Bert, still glowering at Phil as he lowered himself into his seat.

Next door, in the Starlite Lounge, the band started up with a twang of guitars and the rattle of snares. I watched Phil go for pickled eggs and potato chips, and then saw Jack Miller coming over to our table, as though he had been waiting for the chance.

"Ray, I thought it was you."

I introduced him to Henri.

"I've seen you at the gas station," Jack said. Henri just stared at him, didn't say a word. Jack turned back to me. "Come on over, say hello."

On the way across the room, he asked, "Did you find out anything? About Marjorie?"

"I'm working on it," I said. I asked him why he didn't just phone her. "It would be a lot quicker than waiting for me."

"I tried once. Her mom said she was out. And I can't leave my name. I was taking a chance as it was, calling her. Her mother works for us out at the island — she knows who I am."

"I know she does," I said. "I know Mrs. Applewood."

"So I'm counting on you, Ray."

"Marjorie really likes you, that's what I hear." I imagined this was the answer that he wanted to hear. He brightened at once.

Jack and his friends were at a big table near the stage. Besides Radley there were two others; I'd seem them at the Bellisle Club. One of them was dark and wiry and had his own Corvette Stingray parked in the club lot. The other was fleshy and blond. There was no introductions, no explanation of how Charmaine was with them. Boys from the Bellisle Club usually didn't hang out with local girls, at least not publicly.

Charmaine had had too much to drink. Radley had an arm around her neck, dangling over her shoulder. From time to time, he casually squeezed her breast. She didn't look as though she minded it, despite what Chicklet had told us. You could see her nipples through her tank top.

The band took a break and music began to play over the PA system. Jack and Radley were talking about sailboat races. Charmaine looked at me, eyes half-closed. I asked her if she wanted to dance. Radley looked away from his conversation for a moment, the merest hint of hostility in his eyes. He wore a thick gold signet ring on the hand that hung over her breast.

Charmaine said, "Sure, why not?"

I helped her up. She leaned into me, a little unsteady. Her breath was hot, alcohol and tobacco. On the dance floor, I asked, "Charmaine, you think you should be here?"

"Hey, you sound like my mother. I thought these guys were your friends."

"That's not what I meant. What about your buddy over there, in the Tap Room?" I nodded toward the bikers, but she ignored me.

"These guys just want to get laid. You know what one of them said to Clare? He said, 'What's the matter? Don't you Canadian girls *put?*'" She laughed, and then she said. "I know what's going on. They just want to get laid, same as Phil Havelock and that French guy. Same as you, probably. Thing is, some of these American guys? They're, like, real cute. And they're loaded!"

"What about Marjorie?"

"Your new friend Jack put you up to this? How come everyone's asking about Marjorie? She's got a cold, stomach flu or something, is all. You know your trouble?"

"Take it easy. I was just asking."

"You come up here in the summer with your old man, play tennis out at the island — oh, yeah, I know all about it — and then you hang around with these losers from the Shell station." The music stopped. Charmaine lurched into me. "Jesus. You know, Ray, I'm, like, seriously wrecked. Maybe I better get to the powder room. 'Scuse."

She walked toward the table to get her purse just as Bert, the big acne-scarred biker, lurched from his table and cut a swath across the Starlite Lounge dance floor to Jack's table. His boots stomped on the floor.

"Hey, Char, what're you doing with these cocksuckers?"

"Having a couple of beers. What does it look like?"

"You fucking around on me?"

He put his hands under the table and lifted, spilling ashtrays, glasses, and beer onto their laps.

"Hey, Bert, take it easy," Charmaine said. "It's okay, man, really."

The four boys were standing now, wiping the beer and ashes from their clothes. Radley glanced down at the stain on his khaki pants. It was as though he'd wet himself. He looked up. All but one of the boys from the Bellisle Club was bigger than the bikers, and in better shape. Radley lunged, swinging a fist that caught Bert across the chin. Something tore. A wet, ripping noise — the ring on Radley's finger tearing a gash in Bert's left cheek. Bert's head snapped back. He put his hand to his face, saw blood.

"Fuck," he said.

Jack had gone pale and still, but the others moved like lightning. Two of his friends leaped on Bert, all three tumbling to the floor. Two more bikers came running from the Tap Room, pulled the boys off, and pushed them down. Bert stood up, his knife out. The blade flashed in an arc toward Radley's midriff. Radley saw it coming too late. He doubled over. A chair clattered to the floor.

Bert dropped the knife on the table, streaked with blood. Two other bikers kicked at the bodies still on the floor — a flat thudding sound.

"Jesus Christ," said Jack. He took a beer bottle and hit it against the table twice. But the bottle wouldn't break. He gripped it like a bowling pin. He and Bert glared at each other. Bert picked up the knife, held it above his head this time.

"Hold it."

Henri grabbed Bert's wrist from behind. The knife fell to the floor. The bouncer, Spook, materialized out of the gloom and grabbed one biker by the ponytail, the other by the neck. He banged their heads together, then dragged them by their collars fast toward the side door.

With one arm under Bert's neck and one on the back of his head, Henri forced him to the floor. Bert sounded as though he were choking. He writhed like a hooked fish.

"Okay, let him go," Spook said, returning from the exit.

Bert straightened up slowly. He spat blood.

"Fucking animal," said Charmaine Ault.

Bert turned to Jack, the only one of the four who was still standing, and glared at him for a moment. Spook booted Bert from behind, and he staggered from the room.

Radley Smith lay on the floor. In the dim light, the blood pooling on the wood was as black as tar.

| CHAPTER 7 |

People called Jack Miller Jr., Jack's father, "The Congressman." He was supposed to be a friend of Robert Kennedy's, was supposed to have known JFK, and was supposed to be running for the U.S. Senate. He flew his own plane. When he arrived from New York, a man had to be sent the twenty miles to the Iron Falls airport to pick him up. Sometimes they hired someone from town to go. A flurry of phone calls and everyone in town would know he was arriving. Once Phil had done it, driven one of the Millers' big station wagons to the airport. He showed me the crisp, new, American twenty-dollar bill he'd been paid.

The Millers' original money may have come from railways and land development, but the first Senator Miller had managed to stop all development in the area of the Bellisle Club — he wanted it kept as wilderness — and then bought up much of the land himself. He brought influence to bear on the municipal council, and even on the provincial government, some people said.

When Jack's father came striding onto the verandah on Providence Island carrying the ubiquitous tennis racquet, a copy of the *New York*

Times (unobtainable within a hundred miles of Merrick Bay), and a leather briefcase, I knew where Jack got his swagger. He was big and toothy and talked like a radio announcer.

"Glad to know you," he said, shaking my hand. "I hear you're a *great* tennis player." He patted me on the shoulder. "Maybe you'll give me a lesson some time." He continued on through the house. He was here for a meeting with some men up for the weekend, and then reporters and photographers were coming from New York to do a story on him at his summer home.

When his father had gone, Jack said to me, "I guess I owe you one. If it hadn't been for your friend, that lunatic would have stabbed me. Have they picked him up yet?"

The provincial police had arrived at the Shalomar about twenty minutes after the fight, just behind the ambulance, but they had to come all the way from the detachment at Iron Falls; the distance from the nearest police station was one of the reasons that the Black Heart Riders liked to drink there. By the time the police came, the bikers had left. The police knew who they were and had picked up three of them by the next day. But Bert was gone. The motorcycle club had links all over the continent, and the rumour in Merrick Bay was that he'd been spirited away via Sault Ste. Marie and by now was somewhere in northern Michigan.

Jack and I strolled down the path to the front pier of the island.

"Nice friends you have, Ray," said Quentin when she saw me.

"They're not my friends," I said.

Back at the house, Mrs. Miller joined us. She and Jack's father never seemed to be in the same room at the same time; when he entered the house, she left it.

"Let's not mention this to our visitors, especially the people from the magazine," she said. "I suppose I don't need to tell you that. You should never have been in a place like that, Jack."

I turned away for a moment. I was embarrassed, as though it were my fault.

"It's not where people like us belong," she continued. "It can only get you into trouble. Better to stay out of Merrick Bay, Jack. Stay with your own sort."

This was true, no doubt. But it was advice that came too late to be of much use to Jack Miller.

Quentin reached down and took my hand. Her cotton shirt fluttered in the breeze and I could see her small breasts, pale and pink-tipped, beneath. She had a high colour from the effort of the climb, and a sheen of perspiration on her upper lip. A wisp of blond hair fell from the blue bandana she had tied across her forehead. Her hand was dry. The rock face was hot in the afternoon sun. I looked into her eyes, hazel-green. I was hyperventilating. I was frozen. I grasped her hand more tightly.

"Breathe normally," Quentin said, "or you'll start to hallucinate."

But I was already hallucinating. I saw her diving naked into the water. I saw her body cross-hatched by the sunlight in the forest.

"Okay?" she said. "Are your feet okay?"

She was wedged in the bottom of an impossibly thin *V* in the rock just above me.

"You see your next handhold over there?" She nodded to a cleft in the face of the cliff a foot and a half above and to my right. Above that was a rusty spike. I turned. About ten feet beneath me was the broad ledge with a twisted dwarf pine growing out of the rock from which we had come. The waves broke against the foot of the cliff, sixty feet below that.

"Don't look down," she said.

I looked up. The cliff seemed to angle the wrong way, toward the sky and the clouds. I leaned back. The clouds began to spin.

"Don't look at the sky, either!" Quentin yelled.

If I could reach the break in the rock where Quentin was already wedged — a chute, she called it — I could wriggle to the top. The chute angled inward as it ascended, which would make the climb easier.

"Don't look down. Don't look up. Where am I supposed to look?" I asked. I was drenched in sweat.

"Look at me," she said. "Hug the rock."

I put my face against the rock and inhaled deeply, trying to slow my breathing.

"When you get to the next hold, I'll move up and you swing in here. Ready?"

She grunted and pulled.

I had been at the pier loading groceries for Mrs. Ault and the butcher shop, another of the jobs that my aunt had arranged, while Quentin and some of her friends lounged in their boat, drinking from pop bottles they had picked up at the marina. I heard them talking about climbing the cliffs. None of the others wanted to go. Quentin had called me: "Ray, come over here for a minute, will you?"

I put down the loaded cardboard box I had been carrying and walked over to the boat. Quentin looked up at me, shading her eyes with her hand. She asked me if I wanted to go with her to the cliffs.

"Why don't you ask your brother?"

"You've seen him — he's too moody to do anything lately. His father's coming up tomorrow. There's going to be a fight."

"A fight?"

"They always fight."

"What about?" I wanted to change the subject.

"Everything. This time it's because Jack doesn't want to go back to school. He wants to stay up here all winter, if you can believe it. He says he'll live in the old caretaker's place on the mainland, work at the sawmill, play hockey for Iron Falls."

She squinted up at me from beneath her hand. "So why won't you come with me? The cliffs around here are easy. Kids climb them."

"I don't think so."

"Don't have the balls?"

I had fallen only twelve feet, to the ledge below, but it had taken hours getting down. Quentin had to finish the route to the top, come around and down the path, then back to the outboard and over to the island to telephone the ambulance. They brought firemen who helped me down, although, in fact, the descent from the ledge wasn't particularly difficult because of the drugs they gave me — an injection — and because they carried me in a kind of sling.

Quentin Miller had wiped my brow with her blue bandana.

I had slightly fractured and dislocated my left shoulder. The doctor had popped it back in with a snap. I had been kept in the hospital overnight only because of the shock and the pain, and because I hadn't actually arrived until early evening.

When I returned from the hospital the next day, there was an invitation to dinner on Providence Island in Quentin's square, neat handwriting. The note was on creamy paper, with green letterhead and a line drawing of the big house.

"Do you think you should go?" my aunt asked. "There will be drinking. You've been taking all sorts of drugs."

I tried to appear nonchalant. I thought it would be all right, I told her. I would be careful.

| CHAPTER 8 |

The surface of the water of Merrick Bay that evening was like dark oil. The weather had been still and hot all day, sweltering, so hot that my footsteps left prints on the tar in front of the marina. Above the dark shore, the clouds, barely moving, were purple and orange past the setting sun. The weather would break; there was the apprehension of rain. The only sound on the bay was the motorboat, sputtering to life as I pulled the cord. I turned toward the dark shape of Providence Island.

I met Jack on the dirt path up from the back dock to the big house.

"Ray, what are you doing here?"

The pine boughs stirred, the first breath of air. There was an echo of distant thunder.

"I was asked over for dinner," I said.

"Dinner? Are you sure? Nobody told me."

He had already eaten, he said, and was on his way over to the mainland to pick up his father. He seemed distracted, and he looked exhausted.

"You have a chance to speak with Marjorie yet?" he asked.

"Not yet. I thought you were going away for a few days." Jack was supposed to be entering his final year at school, some place in New England; I had understood he would be leaving for a few days to meet the football coaches.

"You haven't heard anything?" he asked.

"Heard anything about what?"

A man came running down the hill behind us. He slapped Jack on the back. "Come on, Jack, we'd better get going. The old man phoned. Pissed. He's over there waiting." I recognized the man as Jack's older brother Stephen, but he apparently didn't remember me from our encounter three years earlier. He was only up on Providence Island for a few days that summer.

I continued up the path onto the verandah and then the hall. No one was around. I looked into the dining room. The table hadn't been set. The house felt deserted. I walked through to the kitchen.

"There you are," said Quentin. She came from behind, took my good arm, and wheeled me around.

"Have I got the right night?" I said.

"This family," she said, shaking her hand. "They don't listen to a word I say. You've got the right night. How are you? Are you all right?"

She didn't wait for me to answer, but turned and led me through a back hall to a side verandah. A small wicker table had been laid out with a bowl of salad, a basket of rolls, and a bottle of wine.

"I thought we'd better eat out here," said Quentin, "away from the main event. It's so hot and muggy, who feels like eating, anyway?"

There was a third place set, and, beside it, an ashtray with a couple of cigarette butts.

"Mother was supposed to be joining us," Quentin said. "Listen, Ray, I'm really sorry about the accident. I wanted to have you out here for a nice dinner, to apologize."

"It wasn't your fault."

"Why don't you pour the wine? Are you able to pour the wine?"

"I can pour the wine."

"Do you drink wine? I mean …"

It seemed to me that this might be a reference to the two years, difference in age between us. The truth was my drinking had so far been confined to beers consumed in the Havelocks' basement or the Applewoods' pump house, and recently for the first time publicly at the Tap Room at the Shalomar. There was never wine at my father's house, and Aunt Beth was a teetotaller.

"More or less all the time," I said.

When we finished the salad, one of the French-Canadian girls from the kitchen brought us some grilled lake bass.

"Jack caught this in the lagoon," said Quentin. "Have you ever been back there?"

In the distance I again heard a rumble like thunder, or perhaps this time it was the Millers' big inboard coming across the water, Jack bringing his father back from the airport.

"I used to go there when I was a boy," I said. "We all did."

"Did you ever hear the Indian?"

The lagoon was at the back end of Providence Island — the swampy northeast end, closest to Merrick Bay, the least desirable end — and it was supposed to be haunted. If you paddled into the lagoon before dusk and sat perfectly still in the canoe as darkness fell, you were supposed to be able to hear footsteps coming through the underbrush.

"Where did you hear about the Indian?" I asked.

"Mrs. Applewood told J.D. He was talking about it at dinner the other night, how he's been coming here for seventy years and he had never heard about it," said Quentin. "So who was he? What's the story, anyway?"

"An Indian fishing guide was supposed to have had a love affair with a woman from Merrick Bay. They were planning to run away together. She was supposed to paddle out to the lagoon at dusk and wait for him there, but instead her husband showed up and when the Indian came out of the bush, he shot him in the face with a shotgun. If you turn and look when you hear the footsteps in the woods — well, when I was a little kid, you weren't supposed to look into his awful shattered face."

"Why is he haunting the place?" Quentin asked.

"He's waiting for someone to come, I guess. His sweetheart."

"When she finally comes, will his spirit be free?"

"I guess so," I said.

"But his girlfriend, she's never going to come. She's been dead a hundred years?"

"I don't know about that part, Quentin. Perhaps he'll be free when someone else comes and looks at him. You know — a conclusion."

"He should just forget her. He should never have got mixed up with someone so different from him in the first place. It would never have worked."

"Yeah, I guess they should have had counselling — Christ, Quentin, it's a ghost story."

"You're the one who said she was his *sweetheart*."

From another part of the house I heard yelling, doors opening and closing. I heard a chair overturn. My shoulder throbbed, and I took another of the painkillers. The air was heavy with the coming weather.

Quentin ignored the commotion and voices from the front of the house. She picked up my bottle of codeine pills and examined the label. "You were a good sport, Ray."

In my family this would have been an insult: the good sport was the one who was no good at anything, the one who volunteered, the patsy. But nothing was more valued on Providence Island than good sportsmanship.

"You're not a bad tennis player," Quentin said, "but I've never seen anyone so clumsy on the rocks. No, I take that back. Not just clumsy, nervous. Why were you so nervous?" She laughed, and then leaned toward me. She put her hand over mine and looked into my eyes and said, "Ray, do *I* make you nervous?" in a throaty voice.

The lame dog padded onto the side verandah, his nails clicking on the wooden floor. He put his snout onto the table between us, scouting for scraps. I leaned toward Quentin and kissed her.

It was silent, now, in the living room. We heard a final screen door slamming, someone walking down the front steps.

"Jack's father, going to see his girlfriend," said Quentin. "He'll be home late. After all, this is probably the last time he'll see her until next summer." She stood. "Let's get out of here, go for a paddle."

I sat on the floor in the middle of the canoe propped up on a cushion against one of the struts, my left arm still in the sling. The pines along the shore had fallen into darkness and the sky was reflected in the lake, an opaque blue. We passed the dark opening to the haunted lagoon, but did not enter. The only sound was the dip of her paddle, then droplets falling into the water and the occasional murmur of distant thunder.

"We'd better find some shelter," I said. "Feels like rain."

"Where can we go?"

"I know a place. Do you have a light?"

She handed me a flashlight with a green and red marine bow light attached. I held the flashlight, and we paddled across the bay past the lights of the village to the mouth of Sucker Creek. We passed beneath the concrete bridge of the old highway. The creek passed so close to my father's house that the paddle flashed in the light from the living room, and we could see inside the windows.

"Is that your mother?" whispered Quentin.

"My aunt," I said. She was huddled over the crossword puzzle at the kitchen table. Everyone in Merrick Bay knew my mother was dead. How could Quentin not? I told her not to speak, to paddle as silently as she could until we reached the edge of the tamarack swamp.

The pump house at the Applewoods' farm was built of stone and mortar, the same stone as the foundations of the barn and the house and the rough wall that ran up behind the farm where the land began to rise. It was a square building with a low doorway, two low, small windows on either side, and a small opening at the back, on the Sucker Creek side. There was a rusty pipe leading out the small rear opening to the river, and another at the front of the building, where Phil and I used to hunt for snakes.

Quentin rammed the canoe onto the grassy bank. I lurched forward, grasping the gunwale with my right hand. On my back I felt the first warm raindrops and heard the rising rustle of the poplars at the river's edge.

The pump machinery was long gone, but there was a wooden pallet a few inches off the floor where it had once been mounted. Here someone had placed a day bed with a horsehair mattress and a couple of blankets. A bed. Someone had even attached some old screening to the windows, to keep the insects out at night. The pump house was much cleaner than I remembered. I wondered who else might have been there.

"You brought a blanket?" I asked.

She handed it to me.

But the night was still hot. We sat in the darkness. I could see only the outline of Quentin's face as I leaned forward to kiss her. With my left arm in the sling, I placed my right hand awkwardly on her shoulder. I was intoxicated with the drugs and the wine and the humid darkness.

She took my hand and guided it up her leg, her Bermuda shorts, my fingers slipping under thin fabric, as hot as the hot, wet night.

"Ray, have you, have you…?"

In the darkness she could not see my answer. I could not see her face. The whine of a mosquito. The rustle of cotton. I felt her fingers fumbling with my clothing, and then again her lips.

"My arm," I said.

"Lean back," she said.

I was awakened in pitch darkness by a freshening breeze whispering against my skin and in the willows, and by a change in the pattern of the rain drumming on the tin roof. I was cold, dizzy, and disoriented. A woman lay beside me. Quentin Miller, her warm arm across my chest. Her breath was sweet with wine.

The tattoo on the roof dribbled to a stop: the storm had passed.

I raised my arm and saw by the luminous dial of my watch that it was four in the morning. I sat up and peered though the low window, moving aside the remnant of blue burlap that someone had hung there. It was lighter outside than in; the clouds, backlit by the moon, were beginning to quicken across the sky.

I crept from beneath the picnic blanket that partially covered us without disturbing her. I pulled my pants on with one hand and tiptoed to the door.

With my good arm, I managed to ease the canoe down the bank and into the water. Quentin came up behind me and put her arms around me, her hands hot on my chest, pressing herself to me from behind. I turned around in her arms and she buttoned up my shirt for me, there, on the grassy verge of Sucker Creek. She helped me with my sling.

"I'm sorry," I said. "I guess we fell asleep. The wine …"

"Ray, don't be sorry," said Quentin. "My parents won't know if I'm home or not. They never come up to our part of the house. They'll think I got in hours ago. My brothers will cover for me. Hey — and I'm eighteen. And for you, it's perfect, this place, the river — you can sneak in and out whenever you like. I'll drop you off as we paddle by your house."

She didn't know about my aunt, who was often on patrol.

"What about the boat from the marina?" The boat I'd taken to Providence Island earlier in the evening was still over there, tethered to the back dock.

"Don't worry," she said. "I'll make sure someone returns it in the morning. One of the boat boys. I'll look after everything. Don't I always? I'm the older woman." Gripping the gunwales, she leaned forward and kissed me.

When we reached the curve in the creek by my house, I stepped carefully from the canoe and made my way up the bank. Quentin vanished down Sucker Creek like a ghost. I ran across our lawn.

Certain evenings after a summer storm, the memory of that night comes back to me, the smell of the earth and the willows after the rain, a freshening wind as the weather starts to clear, the temperature dropping, perhaps the first hint of autumn coming down from the hills, wisps of smoky mist.

Those stolen hours in the pump house played through my mind as the first birds of the morning began to sing.

"What time did you get in?" My aunt stood, her hands on hips, facing me across the kitchen table. But she couldn't deflate my mood.

"Late. I had to wait until the storm cleared."

"The storm didn't end until after three. I know that for a fact, because I was up checking the upstairs shutters."

I said nothing. I shuffled to the stove; I would placate her by having a bowl of the glutinous oatmeal porridge that I normally declined.

"Were you out by the creek?" she asked. She remained perfectly still, but her eyes followed me across the room.

"What?"

"Red clay on the back steps. That's what."

"Wasn't me," I lied. "Must have been from the day before."
My father rattled his newspaper.

Quentin had said how perfect it was, our house being on Sucker Creek, and how she might slip away, paddle across the bay after tennis, some evening perhaps; we would meet in the dark and continue upstream to the pump house.

But now it was past the middle of August, the summer was coming to an end, and on Providence Island some of them had already started the process of departure. The tennis games seemed to be over. Jack's father had gone home to prepare his run for the Senate. J.D. had gone for a week's fishing at a private club on Georgian Bay before returning to New York. Stephen, who had graduated with terrible marks and whose draft deferment was consequently over, had volunteered for some special branch of the military that was meant to guarantee he would avoid combat and had only been on Providence Island for a week. (In the end, he had connived to be sent to Vietnam. He was killed in the spring of 1968.)

Jack, too, was leaving, apparently to join his father for a few days. Then he was supposed be off to his school to get ready for football season.

I wasn't asked to Providence Island again, not the next day, not the day after that, or the day after that.

I phoned Quentin.

"Ray, great to hear your voice. It's been absolutely *crazy* around here, really. Maybe I'll be able to get away tonight. We could paddle up to the pump house."

I waited in the grass by the edge of the river, straining to see into the darkness. But she didn't come. The next night there was a light rain and I stayed upstairs in my room, trying to read. Once I thought I heard a squeaking sound from the river: oar locks, perhaps. I raced downstairs and across the lawn, but saw nothing but the black water moving sluggishly beneath the trees.

I phoned Quentin again. She sounded more business-like this time. In the background I could hear voices, coming and going, the clatter of the breakfast dishes. I told her what I thought I'd heard on the river.

"Not me," she said. "It was raining."

I phoned again, every day it seemed. She would say, "Ray, sorry, I just couldn't — had a bit of sunstroke."

Or, "How's your shoulder, Ray? Shouldn't you be getting plenty of rest?"

Or, "That wind last night, nobody out on the lake."

And finally, "So we're on our way tomorrow, Ray, Mother and me. Heading down to the city for a few days to do some shopping."

"I'll see you when you get back."

"We won't be back. Not until next summer."

"What time are you leaving?"

"Around ten."

I was at the Bellisle Club dock by a quarter to. I waited for an hour and a half — until it became clear that they had already left.

| CHAPTER 9 |

The next night Phil called: a group were going to the drive-in at Iron Falls, then maybe on for an impromptu bonfire and barbecue somewhere to mark the end of the summer. Did I want to go along? I had nothing else to do.

We drove in two cars, Henri in the big pickup from the service station — it had two bench seats in the cab — Phil in his father's Ford, a 1953 sedan, to which Phil had made some alterations: purple passion lights, Hollywood mufflers, and dual chromed carburetors that stuck up above the hood. Accelerating, the car made a noise like a sixteen-wheeler; idling, it sounded like one of the Millers' mahogany inboards.

Phil picked me up at the end of our driveway on the river road. (My father took a dim view both of Phil's car and the Shalomar.) Donny and Marjorie were already in the car. They both seemed sullen; not so strange for Donny, but peculiar for Marjorie. I'd hardly seen her since her party at the beginning of the summer. Donny was in the front seat with Phil, so I sat in the back beside her.

We picked up Charmaine Ault at the store. She said, "So, Ray, how come you decided to come along? Slumming? Where are all your rich friends?"

A snap and a hiss from the front seat: Phil opening a couple of beers.

Marjorie remained aloof. She took several swallows from the bottle of beer that Phil handed back, which was a surprise: Marjorie was known for her disapproval of drinking. She wore the sweet lilac perfume, which seemed to me now to be cheap and tawdry. We leaned into each other as Phil took the curves in the highway to Iron Falls. Marjorie seemed hot, almost feverish.

Charmaine asked, "You decided what you're going to do yet, Marj?"

"No. Don't call me Marj."

"What's there to decide?" I asked.

"The future. Christ, just 'cause we live up here — I mean, we've got a future like anyone else," Marjorie said, taking another swig of beer. I'd never known her to swear. "I'm thinking of moving to St. Thomas."

"Why?" asked Charmaine.

"Too crowded. I hate that dump we're in now." The Applewoods had rented out their house and moved into what used to be the hired hand's house down below. Everyone called it the "black house." It had been empty for several years.

"Why St. Thomas?" I asked.

"I have an aunt there. I could go to business school."

"I thought you wanted to finish high school, go to university," I said.

She shrugged. "I don't know. I might not go. I haven't decided yet."

"So, how's Jack Miller?" I asked.

Charmaine frowned.

"How should I know?" Marjorie asked.

We met up with Henri at the turnoff to the drive-in theatre, just outside of town. He had his arm out the window, gripping the rearview mirror. There were three others in the truck's cab; I couldn't see their faces. Henri gunned the engine as we turned and pulled out, cutting us off and almost hitting us. Phil leaned on the horn — the first four notes of the national anthem in double time — but the pickup pulled to a sudden stop. Another near collision.

"What the fuck?" said Phil.

Henri opened the door, jumped down from the running board, and sauntered up to Phil's window.

"Fuckin' guys won't let us in the drive-in," he said. "Truck's too big." He took a cigarette from the pack that he kept tucked under the sleeve of his T-shirt.

"Where do we go now?" asked Phil.

"Head out to the Golden Dragon maybe," said Henri, "or the picnic grounds? Heard there were some guys heading over there."

The picnic ground was a municipal park in the bush behind Merrick Bay. Being well back from the lake and the rest of the village, it was somewhat remote. There were a couple of asphalt tennis courts, a baseball diamond, some picnic tables, and a concrete barbecue pit, all set off the highway in a grove of pine trees. No one went there much, let alone at night.

"I vote for the picnic ground," said Phil. He turned, glancing at the rest of us. "You guys?"

"You can leave me in town," said Donny. "I'll go down to the pool room. Get home on my own."

"Let's go home," said Marjorie.

"Come *on*, Marjorie," said Charmaine.

Marjorie gazed out the window.

"Ray?"

"Sounds okay to me," I said. I was still in a sort of a Quentin daze, savouring the memory of my night with her, the bitterness of her departure. I was annoyed at her — I hadn't seen her for days; she had gone away with her mother, and she had made no effort to see me — but still, she *had* come with me to the pump house. Marjorie's bare thigh burned against my leg. On the other side, Charmaine's breasts brushed my arm.

Henri banged the side of the car with his hand. "I'll head to town, pick up a couple of cases of beer. Meet you at the picnic grounds."

Phil gunned the engine. Donny got out of the car; he would ride into Iron Falls with Henri in the flatbed of the pickup. Phil reversed in a cloud of dust, turned, and headed back toward Merrick Bay.

There were about ten cars and trucks already at the picnic grounds when we arrived. Most of them had driven around the parking lot and across the baseball diamond and were parked among the trees at the back of the park where they were least visible from the road. There was a fire burning in the barbecue pit. One of the trucks had detachable speakers, which had been put on the roof to provide music.

Henri arrived about ten minutes after we did. Of the other three in the pickup with him, the only one I recognized was Chicklet. He was doing his Johnny Carson routine.

At first, people stood around the cars they had come in, but as the evening wore on, more arrived and a large group began to gather in the clearing around the fire pit. People began to dance. By midnight, there must have been more than fifty people. Someone had a football. We played in the headlights from the trucks. I wandered off to the side, where a few others, singly and in couples, lay in the grass at the edge of the field. We had been drinking since about eight-thirty. I returned to the car.

"Charmaine, isn't this the most fantastic night, the most fantastic sky you've ever seen?"

"Oh, shut up, Ray."

"No, really, it's a wonderful night. Everything works out for the best."

"You always get this way when you're drunk?"

"Charmaine, come and sit in the back of the car with me." I made a clumsy attempt to put my arm around her.

"Oh, sure, right, Ray. It's, like, one o'clock. I'm out of here, getting a ride with Clare. I got to work in the morning. Saturdays are our biggest days. If I'm late my mother will kill me. Keep an eye on Marjorie for me, will you? She's, like, drunk a ton. I don't see you, have a nice life." She leaned into the car and kissed me on the lips.

"Or at least until next summer," I said.

I was exhausted. I sat in the back of Phil's car. Among the changes he'd made to the car was lowering the roof somehow; it was difficult to see out. I opened the door and lay back on the seat, gazing up at the sky.

Chicklet woke me. When I opened my eyes, he was shaking my right shoulder. His eyes were red-rimmed, glistening, darting like a ferret's.

"Ray, c'mon."

"What is it?"

"You want to get laid?"

"What?" I sat up. My head was pounding.

"Yeah, in the back of the pickup."

"Henri's pickup?"

"Anyone who wants it."

I stumbled out of the car. The night was still warm. The fire in the barbecue pit had died down. There seemed to be fewer people around, but there was a big group standing and dancing around the clearing by the truck with the speakers. There were more cars and small trucks parked on the baseball field. Henri's big red-and-chrome pickup was farthest away. Four or five boys were gathered around the truck, as though at the scene of an accident. Both doors on the driver's side were open. The tinny sound of the radio competed with the boom-boom of the speakers from across the field. I saw a bare foot, swinging out the door in rough time to the music. I slowed down.

"You fuckin' believe it?" someone said.

I couldn't believe it. I'd heard about things like this: parties and women who did it for everybody. In my neighbourhood in the city, there was a girl in second year university. Jean the Machine, they called her. I didn't know if she existed.

I was fascinated and horrified. I saw, then backed away into the darkness, and circled into the woods. The forest smelled of rot and dampness. My head was pounding. I stumbled among the trees and threw up.

When I came out of the woods three-quarters of an hour later, the doors of the truck were still open, but there was no one around. She lay sprawled on the back seat, one arm and one leg dangling on the floor. She hummed tunelessly to the music from the radio. I knelt down. Her eyes were half shut. The cab of the truck stank of sex. She wasn't naked; her blouse was half pulled up, as though someone had been reaching underneath to grab her. Her skirt, rumpled at her waist, still covered her. Her skin looked pale and greasy.

She looked up, suddenly seeing me standing on the running board, gazing down at her.

"Oh, hi, Ray." She raised her arm and covered her face with her hand, as though overcome by weariness, and then sobbed. "Ray, I'm cold."

Her head rolled as though her neck was broken, and she passed out.

Henri appeared out of the gloom. "Guess we'd better get old Marj home," he said. I helped him to get her upright in the seat and shut the door of the truck.

That night was the first time that I dreamed of the pump house, hot and damp inside with our heat and the tangled ball of snakes. I woke with a start in the middle of the night, staring at the ceiling, and didn't roll over and back to sleep until the first pink light of dawn.

It was Sunday morning of the Labour Day weekend. Half-filled suitcases lay open in the upstairs rooms as we began the business of clearing out the dressers and cupboards. My footsteps echoed as I walked through the kitchen, because now the shelves were bare. The screen door slammed behind me.

"Are you feverish?" my aunt had asked at breakfast.

At around noon I walked through the bush to the Applewoods' farm. It was the first time that I had been there since the party. From behind one of the old cars in the yard, Donny stood and stared at me. He clenched a wrench in one hand. I walked past the main house to the house below. Marjorie was lying down in the front parlour, her mother told me. She wasn't feeling well.

"I know," I said. "Thought I'd check in, see how she's doing."

Marjorie lay on the couch. "Ray?" She looked at me, then turned away, toward the wall, the back of her hand across her forehead.

"Marj, are you okay?"

She shrugged.

I pulled up one of the hardback chairs. We sat in silence, Marjorie facing the wall. Finally I asked, "Marjorie, you remember what happened last night?"

"I kind of remember. Didn't we all go out to the drive-in?"

"We didn't actually make it into the drive-in, so we drove to the picnic ground."

"Yeah, and I was drunk. And then one of those boys, men I guess they really are — was it Henri? — he took me to the truck. You know, he has this reputation. Supposed to be some kind of *great* lover. Because he's French Canadian, I guess. He's supposed to have a girlfriend, some older woman."

"Dulcy. She works at the Canadian Tire in Iron Falls."

"Like I say, I was drunk. I wanted to drink as much as I could — smoke, too. Maybe it would solve my problem, you know? Dancing around that bonfire, falling down. Getting into that truck with Henri."

"It was more than just Henri. I saw you in the truck."

"To tell you the truth, I can't remember. Were you there, Ray?"

I could hear the sound of running water from the kitchen, a metallic hammering from the yard. I couldn't look at her.

I wondered aloud whether others would hear about what had happened the night in the park — people in Merrick Bay, the kids at the high school in Iron Falls — and if that would affect Marjorie. It was a small place.

"You mean, will I be one of those girls with *a reputation?*" Marjorie said. "Doesn't matter. I won't be here, remember? I'm going away to St. Thomas."

"You've definitely decided?"

She shrugged by way of an answer. I thought for a moment that there were tears in her eyes.

"Is that why?" I asked.

"I guess so." She turned away from me, back to the wall.

"I should have done something," I said. "If I'd done something …"

"What happened last night wasn't … well … it wasn't criminal."

"I guess."

"It was my fault," she said, "if it was anybody's. Nobody made me drink. Nobody made me get in the truck. Nobody made me do anything."

But it wasn't that; it was something else. No one said a word. Had she let them do it? Another of my nightmares for years after would be that night in the picnic grounds, that I had failed her. She had as much as said that she let them do it. But I had let them do it. I had just stood by. Worse, I'd left to go into the woods. I'd done nothing.

I leaned closer to her. I put a hand on her arm. "Marjorie, I'm sorry," I said. She didn't move. "Okay, Marj, I guess I'll see you next year."

I left without speaking to Mrs. Applewood, but I was aware of Donny's eyes on my back as I trudged up the road.

It poisoned everything. I began thinking of that night of sex with Quentin — as the days and weeks and months passed it had become sex, not "making love" — and realized that something about it wasn't right: my arm had been in a sling, painful to touch, immobile, and bound to my body, as though I were half tied up. It had made for a particular kind of encounter: passive, initiated, and stage-managed by Quentin, as though I were a boy being introduced to dark mysteries by a much older woman. I wondered if that was why it had happened, the way it had happened. It began to gnaw at me.

I wrote to her in New York several times over in the fall. People who were in love, who had made love on a summer's night, who were literate and stylish, people like that wrote to each other. I used peacock-green ink. I told her about the books I was reading: *The Great Gatsby*, *A Separate Peace*, *The Catcher in the Rye*. I told her that I was assistant captain of the tennis team and editor of the literary review. I was one of those people whose lives were busy and interesting. In January I described how the snow was up to the living room window, and how the city streets were dark and deep and as muffled as those woods on a snowy evening. I did not ask her why she had not made more of an effort to see me in those last days and cool nights of August before we parted for months.

She replied to my letters only once. She was taking a year off after her freshman year to work at the Morgan Library in New York; she told me about that. She had been in Nassau over Christmas. In New York the weather was cold. She wrote on yellow scribbler paper, in squarish writing, quite unlike the big looping backward-sloping script of most girls I knew. A page and a quarter in purple ink. There was nothing personal in the letter, nothing about her. Nothing about me.

In the spring I sent her a postcard telling her that I had taken a job at the Bellisle Club for the summer. I didn't say that I was waiting for her, but I was.

There was no reply.

PART III

| CHAPTER 10 |

"MIT?" said Mr. McVeen. He was the manager of the Bellisle Club. He held my job forms in his hands. He was dressed in a tan summer suit. He reeked of Old Spice. "You're going to MIT to study economics? So how come you're working in a place like this? Huh? Shouldn't you be in a bank or something?"

The same question had been put by my father. He had wanted me to get a regular job that summer (I was seventeen), but he wasn't enthused about my working at Merrick Bay. He had wanted me to work for a bank, or at an accounting firm in the city, or with underprivileged children in some camp up north to which he gave money, or even to join the army — some summer program they had. I'd told him that by working at the Bellisle Club I would be able to earn money and work on my tennis game, perhaps even get my papers to teach professionally.

"Country clubs," he said. "I don't understand it."

But then something happened which I thought strengthened my hand: his golf game with J.D. Miller. He didn't tell us about it until the night before the actual day, a Saturday at the end of September, the previous autumn.

"You won't be home until after dark tomorrow?" asked Aunt Beth. (In the city, she usually joined us for Friday dinners.) "Where on earth are you going?"

"Merrick Bay."

"Merrick Bay?" My aunt and I spoke almost in the same breath. "At this time of year? What on earth for?" she said. "The house isn't open.

"He's going to play golf," I said. I had seen his clubs in the ratty green bag outside the back door. And so he had to admit it: he was driving up to play golf. With J.D. Miller. At the Bellisle Club.

"Most mysterious," said Aunt Beth.

And so I'd said, "You play golf there," when he'd raised his objections about my working at the Bellisle Club.

He'd just looked at me. Said nothing.

"This is my last summer at the lake," I said to Mr. McVeen (as I'd said to my father). "Living at home, I'll be able to save lots of money." Most of the staff lived in clapboard dormitories that the Club shared with the Merrick Bay Hotel, and for which they were required to pay rent.

"Your family has a cottage up here?" It seemed I'd made a mistake mentioning it.

"Not a cottage, really. More of an old farmhouse."

"You know any members of the Club?"

"One or two. The Millers."

"Oh, I see. The Millers. You know the Millers. Well, listen, *Mr.* Carrier, I hope you don't think this is going to be some kind of big party. You can't hang around with your friends at the beach or the tennis courts. We're running a business here, not a place for college boys to meet their girlfriends."

Chicklet had warned me about this. McVeen hated the summer people. He was a local boy who had made good working for them, and he resented it. Plus he was supposed to be homosexual.

"I understand completely," I said.

"You sure you want this job?" asked Mr. McVeen.

"I want this job. I want to be here. More than anything, sir."

"Don't be a smartass. Report to Schuller in the dining room. I'll be down there to check later."

A pale girl with freckles and wide-apart eyes met me in the foyer. Her name was Cheryl and she was dressed in a gingham dress. Girls who worked at the Bellisle Club were required to wear special uniforms. "Schuller's not here," she said. "He had to go down to the boathouse. I'll show you around, tell you what you're supposed to do. This your first summer?"

"Working here — yes."

"I figured. They always make new people do the joe-jobs."

"How long have you been here?"

"This is my third year," Cheryl said, popping a pink bubble.

My job was to carry out the garbage, sweep the flagstoned paths between the tennis courts, put the white wicker rocking chairs onto the terrace overlooking the bay in the morning and then bring them back inside in the evening, help in the bar, the dining room, and the kitchens. As far as I could tell, I was supposed to do anything that anybody wanted done.

I took the upside-down chairs off the tables. I opened the windows and the French doors to clear out the smoky fug of the night before. I brought crates of lemons and oranges in from the kitchen and cut them into slices and quarters for the gin and tonics and the Long Island iced teas. I peeled lemon zests for the martinis. I cleaned and cut celery for the Bloody Marys.

I was setting up the Snug Bar for lunch. The Snug Bar overlooked the eighteenth hole. Despite its name it was an immense, barn-like lounge, with a stone fireplace. Cheryl was in charge of the waitresses in the Snug and in the dining room.

"I kind of envy you your job," she said. "You're outside a lot of the time. You get to work on your tan."

She asked me if I was going to the staff party the hotel was throwing; they always included the kids working at the Bellisle Club. It was the last thing I wanted to do, but she had shown me around the place and given me gum. I told her I would drop by the dorm and walk over with her.

The screen door slammed; a man in his early twenties came into the lounge. Eleven o'clock in the morning and he was wearing a suit. He obviously wasn't a member of the Bellisle Club.

I asked if I could help, and he said he was just looking around, just passing through the area. Was I from around here? It was really something, this place, eh? Bellisle. Didn't people come here all the way from New York? The Rockefellers, maybe — some big family like that — didn't they used to summer somewhere around here? And the Millers, he asked me, had I ever heard of the Millers? He used to know a Jack Miller at prep school, he said. And now his father was some big politician. The man said he'd heard some story about a fight in a bar; a friend of Jack Miller's — the congressman's son — some friend had been knifed. I told him the story was exaggerated. Nobody had died.

Mr. McVeen came up from behind the man and interrupted. "Didn't I tell you this was private property?" he said to the man. "I told you down at the gate."

"I made a wrong turn," said the man. "Are you telling me even the road is private property?"

"That's right. The road, the parking lots, the docks, the grass, it's all goddamn private property. So get out of here."

After watching the man go, Mr. McVeen turned and asked, "What did you tell him?"

"Nothing."

"What did he want?"

"I don't know. What did he want?"

"I'm the one asking the questions, Mr. Smartass."

A few moments later the lounge doors opened and the first of the guests arrived: three girls in whites who had been playing tennis. I overheard them as I returned to the kitchen:

"Well, she's *definitely* back. Arrived about a week ago."

"How is she?"

"She's fine. Back to normal. Out last night with a bunch of guys at that bar. Farmers or something."

In the afternoon, I was in the kitchen finishing up the last of the lunch dishes. The frosted pebble windows above the scullery sinks were always kept partly opened, allowing me to watch people coming and going up the gravel path from the docks to the clubhouse. I looked up just after the dining room had closed for lunch and saw Quentin. She was with Jack and his father.

I called out to them. They turned and looked at the window. The lake was blue behind them, the lawns green, and the pathways pink. Quentin waved vaguely, as though she hadn't recognized me. I wondered what I was doing there, in the kitchen of the Bellisle Club, grimy and hot. They continued on up the path.

As I stood there at the window in a trance, something hit in me in the face. Pebbles and sand. Phil and Chicklet were outside the window. Phil was working part-time for the hotel garage that summer; the garage had a contract with the club, so Phil was always around checking on the tractors, the lawnmowers, the golf carts, and the pickup truck. Chicklet had started emceeing the dance contests at the hotel and convening the weekly activities night. In the daytime, he rented canoes and paddleboats on the beach.

"Hey, dreamboat, wake up," said Chicklet. "Shalomar, tonight?"

I didn't want to go. I was determined to see Quentin, even if I had to paddle out to Providence Island.

"I can't," I said. "I have to see someone."

"So maybe you'll see her at the Shalomar," Chicklet said, glancing over at Phil. "She was there a couple of nights ago."

"She was? Are you sure?"

I told them I would meet them at the bar.

At dinner I mentioned to my father about the reporter dropping around the bar of the Club in the afternoon, and how the manager had thrown him out. My father looked across the table at my aunt.

"How can they know anything?" he asked.

"Anything about what?" I asked.

"Anything about anything," he said.

Phil and Chicklet were waiting when I arrived. It was eight o'clock and still light out, but there must have been twenty rounds of beer on the table. As soon as I sat down, Phil nudged my leg under the table. I didn't know what he was getting at. He did it again.

"Take it," he whispered. Beneath the table, he shoved something into my hand. I glanced down. Fake ID.

"They're checking tonight," Phil said. "'Cause of the fuckin' cops everywhere." Police cars from the detachment at Iron Falls cruised the streets of the village and the back roads of the district.

"What's going on?" I asked.

"Bert's supposed to be back in town," said Phil.

"The one who stabbed your friend," said Chicklet.

"He's not my friend," I said. "How do you know Bert's around?"

"I heard it down at the garage," said Phil. "Supposed to be out with Donny Applewood somewhere."

There had been other sightings. Someone said Bert had been living at the Allen place, the haunted house. Someone else said they'd seen him in the pool hall at Iron Falls. He had been seen as close as the Golden Dragon.

"Hey, want to know something else? Your friend, the ice princess," said Phil.

"What?" I said.

They were talking about Quentin.

"Get Chicklet to tell you all about it."

"You were there, too!" said Chicklet. His voice was shrill. He laughed. I looked around the room. Was anybody else listening?

Phil leaned toward me, whispering, "The Chicklet here got *put*!"

"No way! Too drunk!" said Chicklet. "Like, I didn't finish before the lights went on."

"What are you talking about? You mean last summer?" I felt ill.

"I mean last *night*."

"Don't blame the fuckin' lights," said Phil.

I hadn't told anyone about my night with Quentin. It was my own delicious secret. Now they were taunting me. I felt my face form a foolish grin, joining in the fun.

"What happened?" I asked.

"She was here. Right here at this table," said Chicklet. He banged the table with the flat of his hand. Then he slapped my arm. I wanted to pour beer on his head. "You should have been here. She was asking after you. She was like, 'I guess you know Ray. How's Ray? Tell Ray *hello* for me.'" He was sort of half doing his breathy Marilyn Monroe impersonation.

"No kidding?" I wondered if he was telling the truth about her mentioning me.

"You should've been here," said Phil. "We all got totally shit-faced."

"You know what she said?" said Chicklet. He hadn't stopped staring at me the whole time, that empty-headed grin on his face. With his pig's eyes and his chewing gum, what woman would have anything to do with him?

"Don't torture him. Tell him how we ended up over there," said Phil.

I had to appear amused while they told their story. Quentin had come into the bar late with a couple of friends. The place had been full and so they sat with Phil, whom she recognized from the gas station, and whom she knew was a friend of mine. Her friends left before midnight, but Quentin stayed.

And the story went on — how they got drunk and stayed until closing time and were the last ones out of the Shalomar. They had walked along the old road back to the village and then up the lane to the Bellisle Club beach. (It was clear from the rhythm of the story that they had told it before, that I wasn't the first to hear it.) They decided to test out the new trampoline that the club had installed. They all got on, jumping together, falling as a jumbled mass of bodies, laughing and falling. Oh, it had been such fun, but then Phil bailed out, because he "thought I was going to barf my guts out." They were hot from the exercise and were going to dive into the lake afterward, anyway. Their clothes were in disarray, and before you knew it there they were nude and lying together on the trampoline, Quentin and Chicklet, with Phil in the pit underneath and so apparently Quentin wanted Chicklet to, she *wanted* him, and she was saying …

But I didn't want to hear it. "I don't believe a word of it," I said.

"Tell him what else she said," said Phil. But Chicklet had paused; the high point of the story was over for him, so Phil said, "She said, 'What's the matter, Jerry? Can't get it up?'"

The two of them were laughing, swaying from side to side in their chairs around that tiny metal table in the urine-smelling, dimly lit Shalomar Tavern. They were idiots, the pair of them, animals, brutes. My mouth was dry.

"I was *drunk*," said Chicklet, "plus the thing was all wobbly."

"All wobbly?" said Phil. "It was your fuckin' *dick* that was wobbly."

In the midst of the merriment, the lights around the trampoline had suddenly come on. Henri LaTroppe was standing beside the green light standard.

Phil said, "He says: 'Hey, can I have some, too?'"

The story seemed like a reprise.

At this point Quentin stood up, steadied herself, climbed from the trampoline, straightened her clothes, walked across the floodlit grass to where Henri stood, and hit him across the face.

"Then she turns — doesn't say a word — walks down to the dock, guns her boat out of there," said Phil.

I imagined the running lights disappearing in the darkness.

| CHAPTER 11 |

Two days later I saw Quentin sitting at one of the white tables beside the tennis courts. She was with the three girls I had overheard talking at the Snug Bar. This time I walked over. She looked up at me.

"Ray. Long time no see."

The four of them stared. I was an insect. I didn't care. I was desperate to talk to Quentin. I wanted to question her. To berate her. To take her up to one of the bedrooms. The things I would do.

"You playing much tennis?" I asked. I stared at her, at her legs, at her bra visible through her tennis shirt. I couldn't believe she had let an idiot like Chicklet, a drunken idiot, lie on top of her.

"What does it look like?" She waved her tennis racquet.

"How 'bout a game?" I asked.

"What, now? Aren't you — on *duty*, or something?"

"Maybe after work. Some afternoon. I could call you," I said.

Out of the corner of my eye, I saw Mr. McVeen coming up the pink gravel path from the clubhouse toward the courts. He seemed to be in a hurry; he was suddenly taking a shortcut across the lawn, which we weren't supposed to do — he was forever telling staff to stay on the paths. How ridiculous he looked, the fawn suit and sunglasses. He walked twenty paces onto the lawn and then called my name from across the swimming pool.

"Okay, sure," Quentin said. "We'll play sometime. Absolutely. Give me a call."

Mr. McVeen had made his way around the pool and now strode toward us. He was close enough that there was no need for him to yell, but he did, anyway. "Carrier, for Christ's sake. Over here, will you? We need some help in the kitchen."

"Okay then, I'll call you," I said to Quentin. As I turned, I heard one of the other girls say, "Is that guy a member, or what? I thought you had to be a member to use these courts."

"I thought I told you — no bothering the guests," Mr. McVeen said.

"I wasn't bothering them. They happen to be friends of mine."

"Friends of yours? They *happen* to be friends of yours?" He stopped walking for a moment so that he could jab me in the shoulder. "Well, excuse me for living, Mr. Goddamn Big Shot. Maybe if they're such great friends of yours, we should just terminate this job right now so you can spend more time with them. What about that?"

"There will be no need for that," I said.

I called Quentin that evening.

"All right. I guess so," she said. "At the municipal courts."

"The municipal courts? You mean at Merrick Bay, behind the picnic grounds?"

"I thought we might try them. I've never played there."

"But they're *asphalt*."

She said nothing.

"Look, I could come out to the island," I said. "We could play there."

"Here? I don't think so."

"What about the Club?"

"I think you're supposed to be a member to use those courts. You know it's supposed to rain tomorrow. Maybe we should put it off a day or two."

"The municipal courts will be fine," I said. "Five o'clock. If it rains, we'll go to the Golden Dragon, have a drink in the front room. I'll meet you there, okay? If it rains?"

"Sure. If it rains. Whatever."

The next afternoon was teeming rain. I drove straight to the Golden Dragon. I waited. They wouldn't serve me liquor so I drank three cups of green tea.

At a quarter to seven, I looked up from my tea and the *Iron Falls Gazette*. A tall, slightly stooped, white-haired man was gazing down at me.

"Are you Carrier?"

"What?"

"Are you Carrier?" he repeated. "Your father is the lawyer?"

"I'm Ray Carrier," I said. "Who are you?" Although I knew he was J.D. Miller. Quentin's father, Jack's grandfather. I had seen him many times on his walks around the island, but I had never actually spoken with him. I was so surprised that I didn't think to stand up or shake his hand. What on earth was he doing in the Golden Dragon? At cocktail hour.

"You know who I am. I'm J.D. Miller."

He leaned his cane against the wall, gripped the table, and laboriously sat down. Khaki pants and a mauve linen shirt, cuffs and collar unbuttoned, white curly hair on his leathery chest. The waiter appeared. J.D. Miller shooed him away.

"I understand you talked to some reporter," he said.

The man in the Snug Bar? That must have been what he meant.

"He was talking to me, is more like it," I said.

"What about?"

"Nothing, really."

"People like us — like the Millers, I mean, my family — we can't be too careful. Did you tell him anything about yourself and my daughter Quentin?"

"About me and Quentin? What is there to tell?"

"You know that we are Roman Catholic?"

Was he concerned that his daughter was seeing someone who wasn't a Catholic?

"You have nothing to worry about," I said. Man to man.

He paused for a moment. "I hope not. And Jack, my grandson, you said nothing about him?"

"Like what?"

"Some fight in a bar?" He paused. He looked at me as though he were sizing me up. "Anything at all."

He signalled the waiter with a hooked finger. "Bring me a Scotch, no ice," he said, not taking his eyes off me. Now he was making some small effort at charm. "You know my son, Jack's father, is planning to run for Congress?"

"Yes."

He took a sip of his drink; there was the tinkle of ice. With his thumb and two long fingers he removed the ice cubes and put them in the ashtray. "And you're planning to go to university in Boston at some point?"

I was surprised he had taken the trouble to find this out.

"I have friends there," he said. "On the board at the university. We give them money."

He picked up his glass and drained half his drink. When he looked at me again, the charm was gone. "We can't have stories in the papers. Surely even you can see that? Don't talk to anyone. Am I making myself clear on this point?"

"Are you threatening me?"

"Yes."

He finished his drink, grimaced, and pulled himself to his feet.

"Is your daughter coming today?" I asked.

He turned, pivoting on his black cane. "I beg your pardon?"

"Quentin and I, we were supposed to play tennis today. She was going to meet me here if it rained. Is she coming?"

He leaned forward and grabbed my arm. "Listen to me, you little shit. You and my daughter will not be seeing each other again. You understand?"

He threw a U.S. twenty on the table and walked toward the door where a man was waiting for him. Through the door I saw the big black car waiting in the parking lot.

Monday morning first thing, Mr. McVeen called me into his office.

"Hey, Mr. Big Shot. You're fired."

"Why?"

"Because I don't like the look on your face. That's why."

I was certain that the Millers had had something to do with this. A functionary like Mr. McVeen would never have acted on his own. I supposed I could have begged my father to intervene, but I didn't really care. My father had been right: I didn't belong there.

As I was leaving McVeen's office, I met Cheryl. She said, "If there's anything I can do … I mean, it's not fair."

But there was nothing she could do. It was only after I'd left the Club that I remembered about the staff dance. I'd stood Cheryl up.

| CHAPTER 12 |

My new job at Confederated Paving (courtesy Aunt Beth, whose ways were mysterious) began the following week. I sat in the back garden dozing, with a novel set in the tropics, a place that on that afternoon seemed not so far from Merrick Bay. The temperature was in the nineties and there was little wind, one of those high summer days when the earth seemed baked and intolerable. In the spinney that trickled into Sucker Creek beside the abandoned hen house, the colours shimmered yellow and green. The electric buzz of the cicadas reverberated into the afternoon (heat bugs, my aunt called them), and the rustle of the aspen in the woods meshed with the whisper of the leaves at the top of the willows on the river bank when even the faintest breeze blew. The radio on the porch droned in the background.

I sat in a white wooden garden chair on the lawn in the backyard, beneath the partial shade of a flowering laburnum that my mother had planted when we had first bought the house. I wore an old pair of shorts, and whenever I became too hot, I strolled through the daisies and tiger lilies at the edge of the lawn, stripped, and waded into the water. The stream pooled here as it curved toward the swamp. The water was about four feet deep, and it always seemed cooler than the lake.

I heard the slapping of the screen door: Aunt Beth coming from the back porch with a basket of laundry.

"What's happening in your book?" she asked as she walked by.

"The husband is cheating. The wife is dying."

"Don't they always just, though?"

I leaned back and closed my eyes to the sun until I felt something wet and warm on my arm. A dog's tongue.

My aunt called out from the clothesline. She was looking past me. "Ray, you have a visitor."

Jack Miller. He was dressed, as usual, in pastel cottons. I was surprised: he had never been to our house before. He knelt down, patted his thigh. "Here, Beau," he called. The dog left my side and ambled toward Jack, the limp more pronounced than it had been before. Jack got up and came over to sit in the other chair.

"Ray, how are you?"

He held out his hand and I half sat up to shake it. The hottest day of the year, lounging in the back garden, and he wanted to shake hands. I caught the scent of something — sweet cologne, Canoe. He must have just put it on; the smell was on my hand.

"Fine, thanks," I said. "And you?"

We always seemed to speak in this stilted way now. It was like meeting a friend of my father's. And then it was though he'd read my mind.

"Your father's not here, is he?"

I thought he seemed a little concerned. "No. Why?"

"Just wondered."

He waved to someone over my shoulder. I turned and saw a blond woman in a convertible backing out the driveway and pulling onto the river road. She had driven him here, and now he was waving her to go on and leave him here in the backyard with me. Aunt Beth stood at the clothesline with clothespins in her mouth.

"How will you get home?" I asked.

"We can walk back to the pier from here. Beau can use the exercise. Just sleeps all day over at the island."

I mentioned the dog's limp.

"Arthritis. Nothing we can do. Also has a minor infection in his ear. I suppose we'll have to put him down one of these days."

He was absently kneading the dog's ear. I felt that there was something he wanted to say.

My aunt came back from the clothesline with the empty basket on her hip. I introduced her to Jack.

"Charmed, I'm sure," she said. It must have been catching: I'd never heard her speak like that before, stilted. "Ray, why don't you offer your friend a nice cold glass of lemonade?"

He accompanied us into the house to get the lemonade, and I was ashamed: the yellow flower pattern of the oilcloth on the kitchen table, the old pump by the sink for drinking water, the patina of brown wax on the linoleum floor (lime-green), the long coils of flypaper hanging from the ceiling. We were the only house I knew of that used flypaper; my aunt bought a season's supply every year at some dusty village store on the way up from the city. I imagined Jack taking all this in, imagined somehow that the Millers actually cared about other people's kitchens, and judged people by them.

"Are you planning to be up here during the winter?" I asked, trying to distract him from observing the kitchen.

He looked startled. "Why do you ask? Why would I be up here in the winter?"

"Something Quentin said, in a letter."

"I didn't know that you and Quentin corresponded."

Corresponded: that was pure Jack Miller. (I didn't mention that I'd only received one letter from Quentin.)

"You can have a beer, if you like, instead of lemonade," I said. "We'll just have to keep it out of sight of my aunt."

"Lemonade will be fine," he said.

We returned to the chairs in the garden, moving them back toward the house, beneath the shade of a couple of maple trees toward the end of the driveway. Again I had the feeling that there was something he wanted to tell me.

"You playing much tennis, Ray?"

I hadn't been asked over to Providence Island to play tennis that summer, as he must have well known. Perhaps the freeze, if that was what it was, was over.

"Hardly any tennis," I said.

"You want to go for a walk?"

"A walk? Jack, maybe you haven't noticed, but it's the hottest day of the summer."

"A dry heat, though."

"A dry heat? I guess so. I suppose you could say it's a dry heat."

More silence.

"So, Jack, why have you come here?"

"I want to visit Marjorie Applewood."

"You want to go see Marj?" I was surprised. It was a summer romance from the year before that I thought was more or less over. I'd heard Marjorie was going away, but I didn't know whether or when she would be back from St. Thomas, or even whether she had actually gone to see her aunt. I said as much.

He assured me that she was home.

"So, if you know she's home, why don't you just go out to the house and see her then?" This sounded rude, so I rephrased the question. "I mean, why do you need me to go with you, Jack? If that's what you're suggesting."

He looked down at the grass, all the time kneading the fur and loose skin behind the dog's ear. He hesitated. "I guess I don't want anyone to see me. Isn't there a way there through the woods? Or perhaps up the creek? I know you can get to the Applewoods' farm up the creek."

"It would be easier to walk if you wanted to reach the old farmhouse," I said. "Especially if you don't want the renters at the Applewoods to see you."

And I think also that he didn't want to see her alone; for some reason he wanted me there with him. I strolled to the house for a T-shirt and some running shoes. When I returned, Jack was at the back of the lawn, staring into the woods as though looking for a way in.

"Listen, Ray, you can't tell anyone about this. I mean, I'd appreciate it if you didn't tell anyone."

"I won't. Why?"

"I'm not supposed to be seeing her. There will be hell to pay if J.D. and my father find out." He seemed to me much less breezy and confident than he had been those first times I'd seen him at Marjorie's and then out on Providence Island.

"Follow me," I said, parting some bushes. The trees here were ironwood, birch, scrub aspen, and scrub pine, with glades of high grass and weeds among them; it had been a hay field only a few years before. The path followed a gentle rise and the forest became older and darker, the smells rich and rotting. We walked silently over a carpet of pine needles. The path led between outcroppings of pink granite, and then we were on top of the hill where my father used to take me to look at the wilderness stretching away to the north. I preferred the view to the west, to Merrick Bay, and beyond that the blue lake dotted with dark islands. In the distance were the flash of a few white sails and the slow progress of motorboats cutting white swaths across the water.

From here we could also just see the immense flag flying on the highest tower of Providence Island. Mr. Miller got one every year on July 4, when they bought a new one for the state house flagstaff. "Ill-mannered," my father used to say. "In a foreign country, you should fly the flag of your host."

A breeze on the plateau cooled us and we rested for a moment. Beau lay on a warm patch of rock, his eyes shut. I pointed to the east, beyond the tamarack swamp and the river winding through the fields, to the two houses of the Applewood farm. Closer to the creek was the big white house with the green roof and wide front porch, now rented out, and, in the distance, the unpainted back house where the Applewoods now lived. The old river road forked at the base of the hill, the main road more or less following the course of the waterway, the other dirt road branching off southeast and into the back country and the big muskeg. We would descend the hill, cross a field, and approach the house from this road.

We scrambled out of the thick growth at the bottom of the hill into a broad valley was beyond the reach of the breezes coming off the lake. The heat was like the steady blast of a furnace. The walk through the field was hard work, insects buzzing our heads, weeds scratching our legs.

At last we crossed the ditch and were on the road. We stopped again beneath a spreading elm, one that had somehow survived. Jack slipped the lead back on Beau in case we should encounter any cars.

The road shimmered in the heat. The only sound was our own footsteps in the dust. And then, in the distance, figures. Two or three, I couldn't tell. Children, perhaps? They seemed to be going on and off the road. Two adult figures: dark wavering lines they were now.

And with them were not children, but dogs. Three dogs running in and out of the ditch water at the side of the road. The one closest to us suddenly stopped, sniffing the air. Then they were loping toward us in an easy trot, like a nightmare of wolves.

I could see them clearly now, their pink tongues lolling. I could hear the patter of their paws on the hard dirt of the road. They were big dogs, farm dogs, crosses between German shepherd and something else.

"Look at those," said Jack. He looked around. "Any trees we can climb?"

"I'd let Beau off the lead, if I were you," I said.

"What?" said Jack, half laughing again, that stilted laugh. "Old Beau? Old Beau won't be able to protect us."

"That's not what I mean. They're more likely to go for a dog on a lead. Beau can't defend himself. Let him off the lead, have him sit behind you."

"What?" he said, hearing something now in the tone of my voice. But it was too late. Beau was at the end of his lead, snarling. The farm dogs circled for only a few seconds. Then they were upon him, the biggest first, jaws locked on the middle of Beau's back. The other two made lunges, feints for Beau's throat, but Jack took the lead and turned Beau by the head so that they couldn't reach him. They attacked Beau's back and flanks, the snapping of teeth like knives. Beau yelped and squealed as Jack spun him around, trying to protect him.

"Jesus Christ," Jack said. "Jesus Christ!"

Two men came sauntering along the road behind the dogs. Donny Applewood I recognized, but not the other: a thickset bearded man with yellow teeth. They both held stubby brown bottles of beer. They wore heavy black boots, jeans, and dirty T-shirts. Donny's shirt hung loose off his shoulders, he was so skinny.

The man with the beard took a last swig of his beer, emptying the bottle. Then he raised his arm and threw the bottle with all his might at the dog that was locked on Beau's back. The bottle struck the dog on the side of the head with a deadened thud. The dog yelped and broke free; all three dogs scattered. The bearded man kicked the dog in the ribs and grabbed him by the collar, forced him into a squatting stance. He looked up. Now I recognized him: it was Bert.

Donny yelled something, struck one of the other dogs, pulled them both behind him.

The dogfight was over. It had lasted about thirty seconds. But there was something else in the air.

Donny nodded at me, a sign of recognition. Then he turned to Jack. "What the fuck are *you* doing out here?"

Despite the heat, Jack had gone pale. "I was hoping to … I'd like to see your sister."

"Well, she don't want to see you," said Donny. "That's for fucking sure."

The dogs circled behind Donny, snarling. On the road, drops of Beau's blood turned black, soaking up the hot dirt.

I turned to Jack. "Let's get out of here. Let's get back to the creek, the lake, and go for a swim."

Jack looked at me. He seemed dazed. He squinted in the glare of the sun. He took an envelope from the pocket of his butter-coloured shorts and handed it to Donny. "Please give it to her."

For a moment they both stood there. Donny snatched the envelope. He sniffed the air, then the envelope. "Smells like a fucking woman." He fingered the envelope. "Money?"

His boots made a scrunching sound on the road as he and Bert turned and headed back down the road.

The colour returned to Jack's face, and then his face became red, livid. He became more incensed the farther away we were from that dusty road, that yellow field, those baying dogs — as though he were angry at something else. Beau strained at the end of his lead, excited and panting froth. We examined him and found several wounds on his back and a couple on his side, but these all seemed to have closed; there were stains on his coat, but he was no longer bleeding. When we reached the fork,

I told Jack he could take the road straight back to the village, and that was what he did.

I called him the next day. The dog had a punctured lung and had developed an infection as a result of the bites on his back, something called subcutaneous emphysema. It could normally be easily cured, but not in an old animal.

"They had to put him down."

"I'm sorry to hear that," I said.

The line crackled, a bad connection. Finally Jack said, "We may take legal action."

"Legal action? Against Donny Applewood and Bert? Good luck. Anyway, you think it's worth it? The dog was old — you said so yourself, almost time to put him down."

"I've got to go now." He hung up.

| CHAPTER 13 |

Within an hour he'd called me back again. He had to talk. Could we meet somewhere? Not the Shalomar; he wanted us to meet where we wouldn't run into anyone we knew. The Red Dragon, I suggested.

When I arrived, the first thing he asked was, "Did she get the money?"

"I have no idea," I said.

It was about his last conversation with Marjorie that he wanted to talk. But I asked him to go back to the beginning. The previous summer.

He'd gone to Ault's General Store two days after her party, when she had blown her top at him and his friends. (That was how she always described it, he said, "blowing her top.") Mrs. Ault was showing Marjorie where to put the chocolate chip cookies; it was a new line of products and Mrs. Ault always liked everything just so, he recalled. He supposed he must have seen Marjorie in the store before, but hadn't really noticed her.

Charmaine Ault had nudged Marjorie with her elbow when she spotted him. "There he is," she had whispered, loud enough for Jack to hear.

Marjorie was wearing blue jeans, he remembered, and a white man's shirt, and her hair was in a ponytail.

"Marjorie, hello. I'm Jack Miller," he said. (As though there were some fantastic possibility that she might not have known who he was, I thought.) "I didn't know you worked here." This was a lie; he had made great efforts to find out how he might come across her again. "If I'd known you worked here, I would have come in more often. Every day. All the time."

When Charmaine heard this, she'd poked Marjorie in the ribs again and rolled her eyes.

After learning she worked mornings at Ault's store, Jack started coming by every day. He offered her ice cream cones when he was buying one for himself. He'd ask if she would like to go for a grilled cheese sandwich and a Coke at the Bay Café, the greasy spoon on the main street. But they only went there once — the waitresses had made too much of a fuss. I could imagine it: Marjorie Applewood with some summer person, a boy! And I could have told him that summer people never went to the Bay Café.

Lounging at the counter by the cash register, the waitresses would have twittered and whispered behind their hands. Jack and Marjorie felt as though they were being watched, which they were, and they never went there again. He started making picnics, of all things, which they ate by the mouth of Sucker Creek. There was a secluded spot there in a clearing behind some poplar trees.

"No," he replied in answer to my question, "I never asked her to the Bellisle Club."

She used to ride her bicycle to work along the river from the Applewood Farm, and he sometimes walked partway home with her, up the old river road as far as the river farmhouse where we lived; he never went farther than that, and he always tried to keep out of sight of any houses or passing cars. (By this time, I calculated, I was already making up a fourth at the Providence Island tennis courts, yet I had known nothing of this.) They always took the path through the high grass on the far side of the creek, he said, rather than walking along the road where they might be seen.

The first time he asked her out in the evening, she said no. "On principle," she told him later. And besides, where would they go? She would never get into the Shalomar and she wouldn't want everybody to know that she had been asked to leave by the Ojibway bouncer. There was the drive-in on the highway to Iron Falls, but the kids from the high schools hung out there, and she didn't want to run into them, either. Eventually she agreed to go with him to the cinema at Iron Falls. She'd told her mother she was going with friends.

She had said for him to come up the drive, it would be all right, she would come out to the car and nobody would see him, but he had said no, he would rather keep it secret. And so, on that very first night, he had arrived early and parked the big Buick station wagon on the road, about half a mile from her drive. They met on the grassy bank of the river in a stand of willows. He had brought a mickey of rum, a couple of bottles of Coke, glasses, and ice cubes.

"Why was it such a big secret?" I asked him.

He shrugged. He said he didn't know why.

It happened the night that he brought the big car, the Packard, perhaps their third evening together, less than two weeks after her party, fumbling on the floor of the black limousine.

He kept telling her that he loved her.

"You told her you loved her?" I had always heard that you were supposed to say you loved a girl when you were trying to have sex with her, a measure of reassurance. "You loved her?"

"I don't know," he said.

And, of course, she had already decided that she loved him. It was better than writing poetry, she'd told him, with a sort of a laugh.

He had unlocked the garage behind the Merrick Bay Hotel and brought his grandfather's big car this time, the limousine, as though he knew this night would be a special occasion, as though something special were going to happen. The car was carpeted, and I imagined that permeating the air inside would be the smell of Jack's cologne, his Canoe, and of Marjorie's sweet, sweet lilac perfume. There would have been tiny lights on the bottom of the limousine doors.

There was no blood to speak of, just the merest speck.

He didn't know what he had been expecting. Did I know anything about that sort of thing? I coughed, looked at the floor. "Not really," I said. I wasn't sure that I wanted to hear all this about Marjorie Applewood. My impression was that men should be discreet about these matters.

They had drunk the usual rum and Coke that night. Perhaps slightly more than usual. I imagined the Coke bottle in a silver ice bucket on the little foldout table that I had seen in the back of that antique car, as though it were champagne.

She had just turned sixteen. Jack was the first man she had ever slept with. "It was great." That was all he could say about it.

While he was telling me this, I couldn't help but think of the evening of the party when Marjorie had taken me up to her room and shown me her poetry, when she had told me that she thought I wasn't like other people. I thought, too, about the death of her father, and the night in the municipal park in the back seat of Henri's truck. And, of course, I thought of Quentin.

And then — it couldn't have been more than a few weeks later — Marjorie told Jack that she had something to tell him. She had news for him.

"Are you sure?" Jack asked. "Are you absolutely sure?"

He couldn't sit down. He couldn't be still. He prowled about in the dim light of the bedroom like a dog before an electric storm, and for this part of his story I could show some sympathy. I could imagine his anxiety. She tried to calm him. She kept checking the door. Her mother was away that evening so he'd come right into her house and up to her bedroom. Donny was somewhere around the farm and she worried that he might hear Jack's footsteps, Jack's ranting. She was sure her brother already knew about her and Jack, about how they used to sneak out together. There was no need to ask Donny to be discreet about their meetings, she assured him; Donny never told anyone anything, he rarely spoke. But there was no point in having Donny know about this, too. There was no telling what he might do. (Years later, I heard about this same evening, the night she told him her news, from Marjorie herself.) And I couldn't help admiring Donny for that; ever since he'd come to live with the Applewoods he'd been a lot of trouble for them, trouble at school, with other kids, and with the police, but he was loyal. Even protective.

Marjorie might have been thinking all sorts of things — about the future, about where they would go and what they would do now that it was true. But she was worried the bedroom light might be visible from the old river road. She got up from the bed where she had been sitting and closed the curtains.

"Sort of taking charge," I said.

"I guess so," said Jack.

Their secret had grown bigger, more complex. Darker.

She tried to calm him, but she couldn't.

"Was it for sure?" I asked.

"Absolutely," he said. (That was an expression the Millers used.) She was absolutely certain. She had been to both the pharmacists in Iron Falls. She had taken one sample in to town herself. She had had her friend Clarrisa take in the other. There was no doubt. And from just the one time.

"I thought you said it was just a little late," he'd said. I imagined that he spoke to her as a child might speak to a parent who had broken a promise.

"This kind of thing was no problem, you said. It's happened before, you said knew about these things. That's what you said …"

That was what she'd said. Don't worry. A throwaway comment as he was saying goodbye to her one tropical night by the brink of Sucker Creek, his canoe bobbing behind him in the black water. But the truth was she didn't know much about these things at all.

Just the one time. In fact, the first time, they calculated.

At first he was unbelieving, and then he was furious.

"How could you let this happen? Why did you do it if you were going to … I thought you were on the *pill* or something? I thought girls were supposed to pay attention to this sort of thing — the *time of the month* or whatever."

Then he'd started to cry, to blubber like a baby. And I believed him: I felt certain he could hardly believe it. He was older than she was. He was supposed to be going to Harvard or Cornell or someplace like that, a place from a storybook, the Ivy League. To play hockey.

He stopped coming by Ault's General Store. He came the day after she told him, but the strain and tension were so great that it must surely have been noticeable to others. They didn't say much; there was nothing much to say — and he didn't go to the store again.

He snuck out to the farm as usual for a few nights after she first told him, then less often, and then he stopped coming around altogether.

One night, as they walked behind the barn, he asked her if there wasn't someone she could see in Iron Falls, a doctor perhaps.

"Doctor? What doctor?" It wasn't a choice that was open to people in Merrick Bay.

A day later he asked, "Why can't someone adopt the baby?" That was all. They never said anything more. The future was someplace else.

Jack had been toying with a plate of noodles. He paused and looked up at me. The story seemed to have come to an end.

"Jack, I'm sorry." There was little more I could say, and I still wasn't sure why he had told me all this. But I thought that it at least helped explain something about Marjorie's behaviour at the end of the summer. Still, for some reason I felt something of guilt, of shame. "I guess it all worked out for the best," I said, trying to lighten the mood that had descended. "Old Marj going down to St. Thomas and all."

Again a pause; he seemed to be searching my face. "You haven't heard anything else?" he asked.

"Haven't heard a thing. Should I have?"

"No, I guess not." He shrugged. "I was just wondering, if you hear anything about Marjorie, how she's doing, if you meet her ..."

But I told him I wouldn't be hearing anything since I was leaving for my new job first thing in the morning. He paid the check. We stood to leave.

"Ray, what I've been telling you ..."

"Don't worry, won't breathe a word," I said.

We shook hands in the parking lot of the Red Dragon. I watched him slouch toward his car in a kind of beaten, tired way that I had never seen in Jack Miller before.

| CHAPTER 14 |

An explosion in my ear. I jumped up in the darkness. Then someone was pounding the side of the trailer.

"Hey, Carrier, you in there, or what?" Lingham yelled. He had fired his gun in the air on the other side of the wall, not a foot from my head. "You want to go shoot some groundhogs or something?"

Lingham was one of my roommates. The other two were older, in their forties, and didn't speak much, at least not to us.

"*Dey no speaka da English*," Lingham said to me the day I arrived. "But don't mention it to them. It hurts their feelings. They might have to take you for a ride. You know: cement overshoes? The St. Clair River? Swim with the fishes?"

They were dark and swarthy and Italian so naturally we assumed they were Mafia, not wondering why the Mafia would have people working on a road repair crew in rural Ontario.

Lingham kept the twenty-two under his bunk. "Don't worry, Carrier," he said to me, stroking the barrel. "Guiseppe and Carlos here, they take you for a ride, I'll execute them. Single shot each to the back of the head. Then I'll chop off their ears and send them to Eliot Ness."

In actual fact the most loathsome thing the Italians did was to take off their shoes and socks inside the trailer. One night, when they were asleep, Lingham carried their socks outside on a shovel and buried them in some tar and gravel, with two little twig crosses to mark the spot. In return they put a dead trout in Lingham's bunk. "Swim with the fishes," they said, making slit-throat gestures with their fingers. They were on to the Mafia joke. It was the one time all summer I ever saw them laugh. (They rarely came drinking with us; they sent their entire wages home to Sicily.) The only other English they knew were a few words to accompany obscene gestures. When a pretty woman drove by in a car, they'd raise their right arms in the air, grab their biceps, and say "Push-a! Push-a!" Then they'd grab their crotches, give themselves a good squeeze, and shake as the car sped by.

"And they say Italians are supposed to be, like, these *great* lovers," said Lingham. "Subtlety, I guess that's the secret. Grabbing your dick all the time, it really drives the ladies wild. 'Push-a, Push-a!'" he said, imitating them. But then he started doing it seriously, all the time, whenever a car drove by. So did I. This was my life. I thought: what am I doing here, shaking my dick at cars?

"Hey, fellas, back to work. The white hats are coming." The crew boss was an old Dutchman, called Dutch, of course. The white hats were the bosses: the foreman (a fat man with thick glasses), the surveyor, sometimes officials from whatever municipality we were in, or from head office.

When the white hats were around, we were silent, sullen, and hot. The only sound was the roar of the burners under the tar, the gritty sound of rakes on gravel. We were hired by municipalities to repair roads that had crumbled during the long winters.

"In the U.S., jailbirds do this kind of work," Lingham said. "Murderers, rapists, bank robbers. Here, they get students to do it." Lingham was going into commerce at the University of Western Ontario, not far down the highway from the town where he lived. "Us and the DPs." Displaced persons, which is what he called anyone who couldn't speak English.

Each town we visited took me farther and farther away from Merrick Bay and Providence Island and Quentin Miller. I wondered about Jack, too, and if Marjorie was back yet. When I thought about Jack and Marjorie, I was aware of an anxious feeling, a fluttering in the stomach.

"How'd you get this beauty job, anyway?" Lingham asked me.

"Through my aunt," I said.

"What — she doesn't like you? She wants you to die young?"

But that wasn't the worst of it. The work was bad, but the free time was worse. There was nothing to do. I read — but what else was there? The fug in the trailers, the nude pin-ups, the cigarette smoke. Dutch smoked all the time, one after the other all day. I asked him why.

He said, "To keep myself company."

Most of the men in our crew — there were eight altogether — were older than Lingham and me. They worked, ate, slept, and smoked. On the weekends, some of them left to be with their families, those that had cars and didn't have too far to drive. I didn't have a car.

We slept in a couple of yellow trailers that were usually parked up some back road, or behind the municipal offices, or in the parking lot of the local depot of the Department of Highways, the places where they kept piles of sand and salt for the winter.

After work, when the others were in their trailers reading dirty novels, or watching the crummy TV or, if we weren't too far from a town, drinking in the local tap room (The Dominion Hotel, The Canada House, The Duke of York) or even at the Legion, Lingham went looking for something to shoot. I had never met anyone who had such a thing for shooting. Anything: birds, turtles crossing the road, squirrels, chipmunks. I'd even seem him standing in the middle of a stream shooting at fish. But groundhogs were his favourites. He would stroll across farmers' fields looking for the holes, the telltale mounds of dirt. He was a great shot. He would wait and wait and wait and then blow their heads off. Sometime he took along a little bacon for bait; they never ate it, but the smell seemed to attract them.

"Then — kapow! They fly apart! Blood all over the place! Hey, and we're doing the farmers a favour."

"You're sick, you know that?" I said.

If he came across abandoned buildings, he'd shoot out the windows.

He loved that gun. After he saw some movie, he rigged up a rack behind the front seat of the car; he could sweep his arm around behind and have the gun in his hand in two seconds. He loved to show it to people. He also liked to provoke people, not fights exactly, but arguments, heated discussions in gas stations and tavern parking lots. He'd insult people, get them riled up, so that they would follow us, jeering, to the car — and then he'd show them the gun, whip it out from behind the seat, like in the movie he'd seen.

"Watch it, the guy's got a gun," they would say.

"Yeah, and he's nuts," I'd say.

"Hey, I only use it for shooting squirrels. Heh, heh, heh," Lingham would say, stroking the barrel of the gun as they backed away.

We were driving away from one of these confrontations when I asked, "You ever actually shoot that thing at anyone?"

"Hell, no. I just like the idea of it. Who doesn't?"

But I had premonitions of violence, and they frightened me.

The year before when I was a student at Saint Jerome's, en route to a Swedish movie, a friend and I arrived at a subway station just as a train was pulling away. We were too late to board. The station was almost empty. Suddenly, three people burst from the train as the doors closed, a skinny man, and close behind him two others. The first man stumbled and fell onto the platform. In an instant the others were on him, kicking. He balled himself into a fetal position. They were shouting something at him as they kicked, we couldn't hear the words — swearing at him — and then they were gone. The man grunted, staggered to his feet. He lurched past us to the stairs, blood smeared on his forehead. He turned to us. "Thanks a lot," he said. We looked ahead, saying nothing. It was like the knifing at the Shalomar.

"So what are you thinking?" Lingham asked.

I was thinking: I've got to get out of here. But there was no way out. Getting to Merrick Bay by hitchhiking or bus would take the better part of a day. You'd have one night's sleep, then turn around and head back.

"Can I borrow your car for the weekend?" I asked.

"Right. And leave me here stuck in the middle of the fucking boonies for forty-eight hours? Just me and the Mafia? Dream on."

As well as attempting to see Quentin, I wanted to get away from Lingham and his peculiar habits. There was the blasting the heads off groundhogs, of course, and the provoking of locals, but that wasn't all. He also liked to blow up frogs and toads; he'd catch them and put a firecracker in their mouths. He always had a ready supply, Cherry Bombs and Super Salutes from Michigan (they were illegal in Ontario). Also bottles and cans.

"Nothing beats wrecking stuff for fun!" he'd say. I would retire to my bunk for a little precious privacy, dreams of Quentin Miller. Then I'd hear voices outside the dirty window: "Carrier's in there beating his meat. Hey, Carrier, you're going to wear that thing out."

And so I would agree to accompany him on his shooting expeditions, or into bars, or gas stations, or to the Dairy Queen.

"We might get laid," Lingham would tell me. "There's cathouses in these little shit towns: Don't think there isn't."

But we could never find them.

We were camped on a dusty road a few miles west of Lake Huron when a call came through for me on the radio in the foreman's truck, just after supper on a Thursday night. I had been with Confederated Paving for almost a month by then. I was slouched on my bunk in the back of our trailer. The rest of the crew had headed off to town. It was payday; they had cash in their pockets. There was a rapping on the window.

"Carrier. They want you in the office."

This was a surprise. The only time I ever visited the office was Thursday afternoon (pay day), and I'd already been that day.

I stepped from the trailer into the hazy dusk of evening. The foreman's office was in the most luxurious trailer — it was actually a motor home. He and Dutch listened in silence as I took the call.

It was Jack Miller. He'd found out how to get in touch with me through my aunt. And he had sought me out.

"Regatta weekend. We need your help." No mention of the dog. All was forgiven. No mention of our talk.

"Big dance afterward, up at the house," Jack said. "Lots of booze. Lots of people."

"Will Quentin be there?"

"She's right here beside me."

A scuffling as she handed him the phone. Then her voice, "Ray, *do* come. It'll be so much fun."

There was static over the radio, a momentary interruption. I thought I heard laughter and the clink of ice in glasses.

"Where are you?" I asked.

"On the front verandah," she said. "Where are you?"

More static, then Jack was back on the line. I told him about the transportation problem.

"Can't help you there. You'll have to figure that one out yourself."

I wanted to ask him about Marjorie, but didn't.

Outside, a gibbous moon hung in the pale sky. Soon I would be beneath this same moon on the wide verandahs of the big house on Providence Island.

"Hey, Carrier, you want to play catch?" Lingham was slapping a hardball into his trapper. It was late and the days were getting shorter now; it was too dark to shoot anything, almost too dark to toss the ball.

"No," I said.

"You want to head into town, get some beer for tomorrow night?"

"You're on your own Lingham. I'm taking off for the weekend."

"Poontang? Hey, get some for me!" He kept throwing the baseball into the pocket of his mitt. Then he suddenly stopped and hopped into the trailer.

"Got something for you," he said when he returned. It was a package of condoms in elaborate and colourful wrapping. People were always giving me condoms. I suppose it was a kind of compliment.

"Open them," he said.

"What? Here? Now?"

"They're kind of special, just for you. There are six in there. You need more than that, and I'll personally make a trip to the drugstore for you. Hey, they know me."

I opened the package, then tore open one of the envelopes. The safe was bright red and was covered with peculiar knobs and ridges.

"The old French Tickler," said Lingham. "Every one in the package is different."

"That's great," I said. "Really great."

I put the things in my back pocket.

"So how are you getting there?" Lingham asked.

There was nothing else for it. He would have to come with me. I asked, "You want to come with me, up to the lake?"

"I get it. Old Lingham drives you. Old Lingham gets to come with you, right? Hey, it's a deal. I'll be there."

But I didn't care. I was on my way back to Providence Island. I was on my way to Quentin Miller.

| CHAPTER 15 |

"What are you doing here?" my father asked. "I thought you were supposed to be in Huron County tarring the roads."

"Don't tell me you've lost your job?" said Aunt Beth. "The second one this summer. I tell you, I can do no more. I wash my hands of the whole thing."

"I haven't lost my job," I said.

They were sitting in their rocking chairs on the front porch, my father in what he called the Port Hope Rocker, my aunt in the iron, spring-hung settee. They had both looked up when Lingham and I pulled into the drive. Lingham was parking the car behind the house, as I had advised him to; I knew that Aunt Beth didn't like visitors' cars to be visible from the front porch. For a moment the only sounds were the squeak of the settee and the click of Aunt Beth's knitting needles.

"I'm back to help with the regatta," I said. "At the Bellisle Club."

"I see," said my father. "Who asked you?"

"The Millers."

"Still at their beck and call, are you then?" asked Aunt Beth.

Lingham came around the house and up the walk behind me, and their tone improved: charm of a kind in front of the guest. But their strange low mood reappeared whenever Lingham left the room.

Clearing the dishes after dinner, Aunt Beth put her hand on my arm. This startled me: we were not much for touching in our family. She gazed into my eyes.

"Ray?" She paused, as though uncertain whether to continue.

"Yes?" I asked. "Aunt Beth, what is it?"

"Do you know anything about this — have you heard anything about what they found?"

I didn't know what she was talking about.

That evening my father came into my room after dinner, something he hadn't done for years. He had something on his mind. He picked up one of the books on the bedside table. *The Picture of Dorian Grey*. He read from the blurb on the back cover, mumbling some of the words aloud: *depravity, licence, sensuality.*

"Nice books you're reading." He paused. "I would prefer that you not have anything to do with the Millers."

"What?"

"You heard me."

"But — why?"

"You know why."

"I don't know why."

"I do not propose to discuss it."

"All I'm doing is helping with the regatta," I said. "They asked, and I said that I would help."

"They are terrible people."

"Don't be ridiculous. You're beginning to sound like Aunt Beth."

"Don't you be rude to me."

It could not have been a better day for the regatta: the sky was bright and there was a warm breeze across the lake from the west that would rise as the day wore on. The man in charge of organizing the sailing events was addressed as the Commodore. He had a ruddy face, a bushy white moustache, and he wore an elaborate braided cap, as though he were the Commodore of the *Queen Mary*, and not merely the Bellisle Yacht Club. Those of us who were helping gathered at the dock of the Club at eight o'clock. This was where the events would be held, beginning with swimming and diving, and then moving into the canoe and skiff events in the late morning and early afternoon.

"Hi, Ray." A quiet voice behind me. Cheryl. The girl I'd stood up at the beginning of the summer. "I heard you were here," she said. "Are you coming to the dance tonight?"

Another dance. The way she looked at me, I should have been flattered.

"No," I said. And then I thought of Lingham. "Actually, yes — at least, I have a date." (Although I hadn't even seen Quentin yet. None of the Millers were anywhere to be seen.) "But I have a friend staying with me. Maybe — well, would you like to go with him, I mean, take him along, maybe show him around?"

She shrugged and smiled. "Sure. Why not?"

The Commodore interrupted, calling me. "I believe you are supposed to be helping with the sailing?"

My job was to help put up the Dan buoys, big yellow balls with flag holders that marked the corners of the triangle for the sailboat races. The races would be run in the big open water to the west of the islands. The starters and the various officials' boats would be based at the T-shaped dock at the south end of Providence Island. I was to report there before lunch. This was perfect; I would have the entire time of the race to myself on the island.

I found a phone booth and called over: "Hello, Mrs. Miller, it's Ray Carrier."

"Who?"

"Ray Carrier. From the River Farm? My father is the lawyer." I remembered that this information had made some impression on her when I'd first met her.

"What is it?" I detected no warmth, no sign of recognition.

"I'm trying to get hold of Quentin."

"She's not up at the house just now. I'll tell her you called." Mrs. Miller's voice had gone terribly formal. She almost sounded British.

"Mrs. Miller, wait. Tell her I'll be over around noon."

"Excuse me? You'll be over here?"

"I'm helping with the races."

"I see," she said. She hung up.

We left for the open waters of the lake at about ten o'clock. We followed another boat, skippered by an official with charts and a compass, who instructed us where to drop the markers. We dropped yellow line from spools fixed to the boat. The deepest, the point of the triangle closest to Providence Island, was about sixty feet, and it took us some time to secure the anchors. The wind rose steadily as we worked.

Back at the island dock, I saw Jack speaking with Mrs. Applewood. She was wearing the white and grey nurses' uniform that J.D. liked her to wear. She had just stepped from the green rowboat. The garbage boat. She used it to row herself over to the island on the days she worked.

"How is Marjorie?" Jack asked her.

Mrs. Applewood didn't answer.

Jack moved away from her, shrugging. He joined the regatta officials at the foot of the dock. He held a wooden clipboard. He grimaced at me as he passed, perhaps as though I should understand what this was all about. I didn't know where things stood between him and Marjorie.

"Going to watch the races?" I asked Mrs. Applewood.

"I've got something else to do," she said. She glared at me. "Lunch for old Mr. Miller."

She seemed to have shrunk since I last saw her. She turned and walked up to the house.

I recalled (at least I think I remembered — I didn't think I was imagining this) on that late, still Saturday afternoon in August the green rowboat gliding away from me across the black water and into the shadows at the back of Providence Island, the oars dipping and squeaking, the stern low where J.D. Miller sat in his white ducks, his tennis sweater, the big straw hat, his black cane across his knees. Mrs. Applewood, dressed in the ridiculous grey dress with the white apron that they insisted she wear, sat in the middle, at the oars, a little toward the bow. It was hard work rowing that boat; it was heavy and beamy, and was supposed to be stable in rough water, the reason they used it to ferry old J.D. Miller around. But there was no rough water here: the burgee hung limp in the dead air of the lee of the island. Only an occasional rush in the tops of the tallest trees told of the high winds rising to the west. I stood on the dock. I was waiting for Quentin. I waved as they disappeared around the curve of the dark side of the island. They didn't wave back. The old man hadn't said a word to me, had refused my hand when I offered to help him into the boat.

This would have been about an hour after that brief conversation with Mrs. Applewood on the path.

I interrupted Jack who was giving instructions to some of the others: "Where's Quentin?"

"She's with some guy over on the mainland," he said. "They're going out to watch the sailing races, should be back around three."

By four o'clock the events on the mainland were over and the sailboat races were finishing. The wind had been rising all afternoon. Boats were coming around the point in disarray, lines and halyards snapping, their sails rippling, the crews soaked.

I was at the back boathouse, waiting. I had been waiting for Quentin for over an hour. Now I was preparing to cast off one of the big outboards, to go around to the west side and check for the boats coming in; we would take up the markers as soon as the last race was over.

But something was wrong.

Outboards were roaring across the channel from the mainland. On the big dock, I could see that people were gathering in small groups, gesticulating, pointing out to the lake. There seemed to be yelling, but I couldn't hear what. The words were lost in the rising wind.

A figure left the group and approached me, running along the path from the point. I saw her golden hair blowing in the wind. Quentin Miller. I stood with my hands on my hips (with a foolish smile on my lips no doubt). I supposed that she had at last come to find me.

But there were no words of greeting.

"Where's my father?" she asked.

"What?" For a moment I was confused about who her father was.

"J.D."

"He's out watching the races in the green rowboat. With Mrs. Applewood."

"They're not back yet," she said.

"I haven't seen them."

"They were supposed to be back by four o'clock to get ready for the presentations."

I knew that J.D. always came over to the mainland for the closing ceremonies. He donated half the trophies and liked to present the prizes. His progeny were usually prominent among the winners.

"You want me to go out in the boat and look?" I asked.

"Already lots of boats out looking. And it's wild out there. No, you look along the shore. Take the path. Look in the lagoon, the old steamboat cribs, around the other side, to windward. Look there."

I made my way along the path, running where it wasn't overgrown or obstructed by fallen trees. I walked along the muddy shore of the lagoon and then, back on the path, continued toward the north of the island where I judged the sunken steamboat pier cribs to be. I could see nothing. I raced across the island to the far side, to the summerhouse, a gazebo that stood high on the western cliffs overlooking the lake.

There had been wispy clouds on the horizon all day, but now a change was coming. The wind had shifted from the west to the northwest and was blowing almost out of the north. Around the summerhouse, the wind howled. The light had changed, making the whitecaps menacing, the water grey. Sheets of rain were advancing across the lake. I knelt and crawled toward the edge of the bluff, peering over. I was mesmerized by the boiling foam as the waves crashed into the rocks below. My eye followed the shore of the island up toward the point, where the bluffs melted away to a few, stunted, wind-swept pines. A figure. A hunched shivering figure in white and grey.

It wasn't anyone's fault. He was an old man, a cripple. He should never have been out on the water in weather like that in the first place, but he had insisted — there were many who had heard him shouting — he had insisted that he have his way on that day as he had on many others. He wanted to watch the sailboat races. He wanted to be rowed around the back of the island, past the boathouses and the lagoon and the old steamboat pier, built there where the deep water began, and then around the northern tip of the island to the western side, into the prevailing wind and the waves. He didn't care how much work it was for Mrs. Applewood rowing that old green boat. He wanted what he wanted.

And, of course, it was her job. She was his companion and was paid to do that sort of thing.

The gardener, someone, had heard her at the dock. "I can manage," she had said. "It's perfectly all right. I can manage."

They had left the docks and headed north, up along the eastern side of the island, where the water was dark and smooth. I had seen them myself.

"He wanted to see the sailboat races," she kept saying, afterward, when we picked her up, drenched and shivering, just on the wild side of the point.

"But it was too rough," people said. "And you couldn't really see the sailboat races from there, anyway, not if you kept close to shore. The boats were too far out in the lake to see much from there ..."

"And it was long past two o'clock when they left, the races half over."

"Wouldn't he have known that?"

"Wouldn't *she*?"

"Try telling that old bastard anything, and he wanted to go."

"It's true," I said. "He wanted to go out in the boat."

"The woman is incompetent," said Mrs. Miller. "Why he always wanted her around, I don't know. We should never have let her out of the kitchen."

The search for the boat and the body of J.D. Miller continued until dark. Nothing. Even after that, a few boats kept a search along the shore of the island, their spotlights combing the shaggy undergrowth at the water line for signs of the accident. But it was hopeless. The wind kept up, raging through the night, sometimes mixed with pelting rain. The next day dawned dim and cool under low scudding clouds. The search resumed. Big police boats the likes of which we had never seen in Merrick Bay came from the foot of the lakes. Searchers tramped along the shore of the island. A small plane passed to and fro, droning in the sky above Merrick Bay and then, in the afternoon, a helicopter came.

On Saturday night we ate dinner late. The air was electric at my father's house, something suppressed.

"Some old guy drowned," Lingham said. The man was utterly clueless.

"We heard," said my father.

But my father and my aunt didn't seem to want to follow up, to ask questions. They didn't wish to speculate about what had happened, like most other people did.

I told them, anyway.

"Mrs. Applewood says the boat was swamped about fifty yards out from the point. She'd wanted to stay close to shore, but he insisted. She said, 'You know what he can be like.'"

"I do know," said my father.

"She tried to save him," I said. "She tried to pull him ashore, but he sank from sight almost at once. So did the old boat. That's what she said."

"So you think they'll find the corpse?" asked Lingham. The idea seemed to brighten him. He took a celery stick from the little bowl in the middle of the table. My aunt prepared these when we had guests for dinner, but no one ever touched them. No one except Lingham. He snapped them in half and crunched loudly.

My father regarded him in silence. When Lingham's crunching had subsided, my father said, "Fifty yards out, that's where the bottom drops off. They'll never find him. The body may surface next spring, after the ice goes out."

The next day, Sunday, many people went to visit the Millers, offering their condolences. My father, instead, visited Mrs. Applewood.

The people of Bellisle were shocked by the drowning (the "disappearance," as it would come to be called) of J.D. Miller, of course, as were the people of Merrick Bay, but there didn't seem to be much real sorrow. He was an old man, and the truth was that no one had much liked him. Even the family seemed dry-eyed; his daughter-in-law, Mrs. Miller, had remained business-like throughout.

But they were still affected. He had been with them at lunch; he had toured the docks after that, stopping in at various events. Now he was gone. Vanished forever.

Not Lingham. He knew none of them, and he was quite detached.

Chapter 15

"Maybe she pushed him over the side," he said. We were in the car, on the way back to work on the roads of Huron County. "Maybe they were lovers. She says, 'No more nookie, you're too old and wrinkly and gross,' so then he tries to rush her, you know, goes for her tits. I bet that's what happened. So she cracks him over the noodle with the oar and pushes him overboard. That's the way I see it." He gazed out the window at the farmland passing by. Then he started to whistle.

His whistling irritated me, so I asked, "How was your date with Cheryl?"

"Really nice," he said.

"Nice?"

"Yeah, nice. She's a really nice person. You know — thinks about other people's feelings. Nice. What? Why are you looking at me like that? She's nice. Is that so strange?"

Several minutes' silence. Then Lingham said, "She gave me her address, you know? I'm going to write her a letter. Never done that before, written a letter to a girl, like, for no reason, no *ulterior motive*. Have you? You ever written letters to a girl?"

"Yes," I said.

"Oh, yeah? Who?"

"I'd rather not talk about it," I said.

Lingham started whistling again.

A few days later (so I heard), one of the oars turned up in the lagoon. And a week after that they closed the big house on Providence Island. Quentin returned to New York City. Because of the disaster, my connection with her (however tenuous it had been) was over, at least for the time being. I didn't see her again for five years.

The next year I took a summer job out west, near Banff. I wouldn't return to Merrick Bay for twenty-three years.

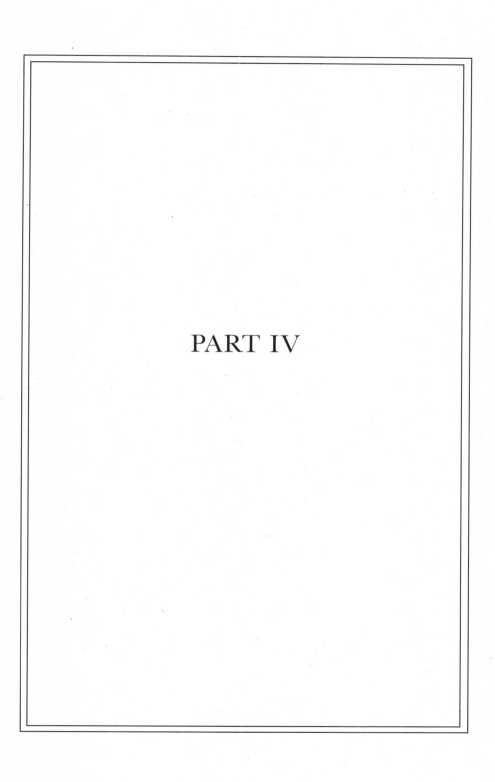

PART IV

| CHAPTER 16 |

The rumour was that the pension fund of German Railways was investing in Merrick Bay. That was the reason for the yellow bulldozers parked on the mud flats back from the mouth of Sucker Creek. Holiday condominiums. So Aunt Beth said.

"Who will live in these condominiums?" I asked.

We were on our way to the Merrick Bay Hotel for the reception following my father's funeral.

"Old people," Aunt Beth said. "It will be what they call a 'golden age' community."

"But it's not even on the water."

"They want to build a waterway to the lake," she said. "Some kind of canal, so that you can see your boat from your living room while you're watching TV. Like in Florida."

On the cliffs south of the village — cliffs that we had always thought too high, too steep, and too far from the water for cottages to be built — there were now elaborate houses of cedar and glass, cantilevered and suspended over the water, the kind of houses you saw on the West Coast, high above the ocean. I had seen pictures of these places in magazines.

"When did they sell that land by the cliffs?" I asked.

"Ten, fifteen years ago. Not long after the Millers were divorced. Just as well. Children used to climb there. There were some nasty accidents. I suppose I don't need to tell you that." She shook her head, gazing out the window.

We turned off the old river road and drove along the curve of the bay. We were at the head of the procession, in Aunt Beth's elderly Plymouth. The funeral home had offered to provide a car for Aunt Beth and me, as the immediate family, but she had told them that there was no need; it was costing enough to have the hearse come all the way from Iron Falls to St. Andrew's United and back again. The undertaker had discreetly suggested that my aunt might at least like a driver after the service, as she might be in a state of some emotional stress.

"I'll be fine once the hymns are over," my aunt had told him. "That is the point of the hymns — to get all that business out of your system."

We had selected "Abide With Me," "Eternal Father, Strong to Save," — when I questioned my aunt about this choice, she said, "Never forget, your father spent five years overseas. You can imagine what he thought about Germans coming to Merrick Bay and building condominiums" — and "Praise My Soul the King of Heaven," which was played while the undertaker's men wheeled the body from the church and back into the waiting hearse.

"Besides," she had told the man, "I have my nephew. He can drive me to the hotel."

During the service, the minister read from Psalm 18:

> The Lord is my rock, and my fortress, and my deliverer;
> my God my strength, in whom I will trust; my buckler,
> and the horn my salvation, and my high tower.

"What is a buckler, anyway?" I asked my aunt.

"A kind of breastplate. Like knights of olden times wore."

"Why did he select that one, do you think?"

"Because I asked him to," said Aunt Beth. "It was one of your father's favourites."

"One of his favourites?" My father wasn't even religious.

My aunt looked sideways at me. "He was more complicated than you think."

And it was true that I had never understood my father to be a man of passion or particular moral complexity. He was a character to me, a type — and a rather dry type at that. His parents were Scottish. His father, his grandfather, and that man's father before him had all been legal clerks, civil servants of some kind in Edinburgh, who held for generations the same position — Signet to the King's Bench. It was as though they were of a particular caste — minor civil functionaries. His own father had left Scotland in rebellion and come to Ontario. My father had broken from this pattern to become an independent professional, a small-town lawyer. He had picked for himself a narrow, stony path, and he had stuck to it.

Travel and the arts held no interest for him. Such choices were only for the wealthy, for the broadly educated. Among the worst terms of opprobrium for him were *wastrel* and *dilettante* and *poseur*. He was not himself a churchgoer, but both his parents had been — his father a Presbyterian, his mother a Catholic — and this had had an influence. He held strong views. He never referred to unorthodox personal or sexual arrangements. See no evil.

When he was young, he had received a small inheritance; rather than travel to France or the South Seas, or buy stock and bonds, he used the money to retire his mortgage, buy the small building from where he ran his practice, and send me to Saint Jerome's and then to college. He was a strong believer in education and personal responsibility. It went with his horror of laxity.

By the time I was sixteen, I had him firmly classified. I could imitate his walk, his talk, his views on real and imaginary subjects, and did so for the amusement of my friends at St. Jerome's.

Now I thought I knew better. I used to think of his lawyer's duties as little more than a functionary's — helping with wills and estates; it was in the genes, after all — but now I thought that with the Applewoods, and perhaps with others, his duties wore more akin to those of a priest.

He held those secrets about Marjorie and Jack and later J.D. Miller in his heart for his whole life. He wanted people spared.

In the end we had decided to have my father cremated. This avoided the need for securing a plot and for "driving all over the countryside so that we may have a grave side scene," as my aunt said. If we wanted to put up a headstone somewhere for the ashes, that could be done in due course.

"Perhaps we'll put the ashes in your father's vegetable garden," she said.

"Or in Merrick Bay," I said.

"I don't think so. He was never a strong swimmer. And surely that would be in doubtful taste, considering the circumstances."

We drove past the brown cattails through which my father had walked into the water. Having dawned bright and hot, the day had now turned grey, a spring storm coming in from the southeast, and there was a slight chop on the bay. The water remained low; the lake bottom was a wasteland, pocked and brown, like another planet. No one had ever seen the bay like this, and it cast a pall. Things had been surfacing, uncovered by the low water and the movement of currents: old tires, bicycles, a ringer washing machine, a stove, boats, and pieces of boats.

"Perhaps the old yellow canoe will turn up," said Aunt Beth. It had gone missing over the winter. "Everything else is turning up."

The Merrick Bay Hotel was a long two-storey affair of white clapboard, with towers at either end and a covered verandah across the front that faced the lake. The main entrance was beneath a large portico at the rear. The hotel had been built in the 1920s and had been owned by the same family until the late 1970s. It had then quickly gone through a series of owners and was rumoured to again be on the brink of receivership. The vegetable and flower gardens had been cut back, and up close you could see that the whole place was badly in need of paint.

The lobby was faded pink — the walls, the curtains, the carpet — and all the reception rooms smelled of old wood and musty bedding. At the door to the lounge, a long table was laid out with sandwiches, cakes, tea, and coffee. Here my aunt and I took our places, awaiting the arrival of the guests. The minister from Nova Scotia came first.

"A lovely service, I thought," he said, "and the first we've had at Saint Andrew's in over a year. So nice to see the church getting some use. Oh, I hope I haven't said the wrong thing."

After twenty minutes, the small lobby was jammed, and my aunt and I gave up formally greeting the guests; we were both tired. As I drifted into the lounge, a large woman with a weathered smiley face came up to me. "Ray Carrier. You don't remember me. Charmaine Wilson. Charmaine Ault. My mother said she'd seen you."

When I had accompanied my aunt up the aisle that morning, I'd been surprised to find the church full. The small group I'd expected — grey-haired aunts and uncles, a few cousins, friends, colleagues from my father's days in the city, a few lawyers from his firm, even a couple of army types — were huddled at the front. But what was surprising to me were the local people who had come; there were more of them than there were of my father's friends and family. My father had become unknown to me.

"Yeah, I knew your dad," Charmaine said. "Way longer than I ever knew you, matter of fact. He's been living here more or less year-round for, what, coming on ten years? God, when did I last see you? More than twenty years ago? What do you do now, anyway? Some kind of engineer? That's what your aunt said."

I told her I designed and helped sell conveying equipment, although I wasn't actually an engineer.

"No kidding? I work at the store, on and off, same as always. Anyways, you don't look any different. You married?"

"Seven, eight years ago. It's over now."

"I always thought you might end up with that girl from out Providence Island. You liked her. That's what everybody said. She was beautiful — I'll give you that. Snotty, though. Had a funny name."

"Quentin."

"Only Quentin I ever heard of. And older than you, too, eh? Then all that funny business. Course, nobody knew anything then. You know she's been around here, a month or so back, talking to the government people at Iron Falls? Leastways, that's what I heard. They're selling that place. Yeah. Hey, and what about that old rowboat? And your dad, I mean. I seen him, like, maybe half an hour before it happened? Came into the store, same as usual, gets his papers? Then they find him lying in the grass beside that damn boat. I mean, Jesus!"

"Amazing the boat didn't turn up before this," I said. "They looked all over at the time."

"Stuck in the cribs all these years, that's what they think," said Charmaine. Her eyes were bright. "Phil Havelock told me they think they must have run into one of the footings from the old steamer dock at the time, and that's when he drowned. That old garbage boat was always waterlogged, anyway — would sink straight to the bottom." She showed how with her hands. "Boat must have been caught in the crib for years, then broke loose and been shifting her way toward the shore ever since."

From across the room, my aunt beckoned. She stood next to a vaguely familiar figure. I saw that it was Mrs. Harris, my father's former lady friend. English. My aunt wasn't fond of Mrs. Harris, didn't like what she called her airs and accents. I excused myself from Charmaine to rescue her. I thanked Mrs. Harris for coming all this way. She waved her hand in dismissal.

"Of course, I had to come. I was at one time very attached to your father. In love, one might almost say."

"I didn't know …"

She saw I was embarrassed. "Besides, I had to see where he lived all these years. That little house on the river. Do you know, I've never been to Merrick Bay? I was at the Bellisle Club once years ago. Those big summer homes, so expensive! Now I think they might be rather a buy."

"You're interested in property here, Mrs. Harris?"

"Actually I'm in real estate. And I know what you're thinking — interest rates where they are, surely the bottom's dropped out of the market. And you'd be right. But do you know what?"

"What."

"Opportunity!" said Mrs. Harris. "Great time to snap up bargains. Do you think there's any chance your aunt's going to sell? You have water access."

"Sucker Creek? Is that what they call it now, water access?"

And now my aunt returned the favour, and taking my elbow, rescued me from Mrs. Harris.

Half an hour later I left, exhausted. (In Ketchum, the night before I flew out, Katie had warned me about this: I'd be knocked out, she'd said, and I should take time off to rest after the funeral.) I told my aunt that I would be waiting in the lobby. I walked through the kitchens and lit a cigarette. A resort hotel and you weren't allowed to smoke. No wonder they were going bankrupt. I left the hotel and walked up the path through the old vegetable gardens, now gone to weeds, to the service station behind the staff buildings. It was tiny by modern standards, a museum piece with its wooden siding and mullion windows, a portico over the pumps. A boy of about twenty looked up from the counter when I opened the door. He had dark hair that he was already starting to lose. I was always amazed by the likeness of children to their parents. He wore coveralls with the name Kevin stitched in red on a blue oval above the breast pocket.

"Your father here?" I asked.

Phil Havelock came in from the bay where he had been working underneath a big car that seemed to fill the garage. He wiped his hands on his jeans. He was large and bald.

"Sorry to hear about your dad."

We shook hands. I was beginning to find the reunions unnerving. And I thought he might have come to the funeral.

"So, this is your place," I said. "How's business?"

"Here? So-so. But I also own the new place out on the highway. It's a gold mine."

"The highway widening. All these new houses. And you're on the town council."

"Reminds me — let me show you something."

He led me out the door of the office and into the garage. He flipped the switch. "Remember that?"

The 1942 Packard. We used to gaze at it through the windows of the Millers' locked garage. The car gleamed under the lights.

"You want it?" asked Phil. "It's for sale. Been working on it over a month. Probably going south to auction in a couple of weeks."

I ran my hand along the burnished fenders. The last time the car had been out was probably the time J.D. Miller took my father golfing.

"You want to join me for a quick drink at the hotel?" I asked.

Phil shook his head. "Can't. Gave up years ago. But I also own the cab." I had noticed an old station wagon beside the garage. "The only cab in town. Another gold mine, even when I have the kid here driving it. Why don't I give you the guided tour? We can talk on the way."

I told him I had to drive my aunt home; after the reception, a few relatives were coming over for tea. I asked him about the Providence Island rowboat.

"Yeah, they got that old piece of shit down at the marina," Phil said. "Big hole in the bottom. They really ran into something."

| CHAPTER 17 |

The kitchen windows were open wide to the evening air, warm before the storm and sweet with the smell of the damp earth and pine needles. Something about that kind of weather in the lakes — the air electric with expectation — reminded me of my youth. We didn't have days like this where I lived in Idaho; it was a landscape of grey and brown.

I helped my aunt clear away the tea things. Her mood was stony. I think we were both a little annoyed with each other for not having been more upset about my father's death. It revealed something about us, a stolidity in our little family that was supposed to have been stoic and admirable, but that may have just been a kind of coldness, after all.

"What are your plans?" she asked.

I had no plans, certainly no plans for leaving Merrick Bay; I was delaying my business meetings in the north. I was hoping to see Quentin Miller again. Aunt Beth had been right about that.

But I couldn't linger indefinitely, not just because of Quentin Miller. There was something else. I was growing curious: I wanted to find out what my father had been doing that grey morning. I had suspicions.

"What about the way he died?" I asked.

"Some things are better left undisturbed," she said.

When I had returned from driving one of the guests back to the hotel after tea, there had been a telephone message, someone from the marina. The yellow canoe had been spotted in the marshy lagoon at the north end of Providence Island. Aunt Beth didn't know exactly when during the winter the canoe had gone missing. It was normally kept overturned on the bank of the creek at the edge of our property, fastened to a tree by a length of old plastic clothesline. It had likely been carried down the creek during spring.

At the marina I rented an aluminum boat with a small outboard motor. The boat was tethered to a floating dock at the end of the pier. Both the dock and the boat bobbed in the waves.

"Better hurry," said the man at the gas pumps. "Storm coming. Though we can use the rain, that's for damn sure." He gazed out at the black bay.

Because of the low level of the lake, at the mouth of the lagoon I had to pull the motor up and pole across the sandbar. Inside the lagoon, the surface was still. Only the tops of the fir trees rustled in the wind. I saw the canoe floating upside down near the shore, surrounded by branches and deadheads. I nosed toward it and shut off the outboard. Footsteps. Footsteps through the brush ... the branches of a fallen, half-floating tree brushed rhythmically against the boat. The lagoon was always filled with debris — felled trees, driftwood, deadheads lurking beneath the surface, the wreckage of docks broken by the winter ice. Debris floated in and couldn't get out; rowboats and canoes and sailboats that had escaped their moorings often turned up in the Providence Island lagoon.

I worked a rope around the bow strut of the canoe and revved the motor in reverse. The outboard bobbed back and forth in the roiling water as though attached to an anchor. Suddenly the canoe came free with a lurch, the stern pulling from the mud with a loud sucking noise and a sheaf of slimy branches. The canoe wallowed in the black water of the lagoon, the stern low as though caught on something. I would have to right the canoe to get it over the sandbar at the mouth of the lagoon. I cut the motor and began pulling the rope. The splayed green-and-black stump of a deadhead squeaked, rubbing against the side of the canoe. The clothesline was tangled in the branches. I reached into the icy water to pull it clear. The limbs of the stump looked like human limbs floating up, like the blue hand of Mr. Applewood beneath the downed willow tree. Rain began to fall, breaking the mirrored surface of the lagoon. I couldn't see the rope in the roots. I pulled my aching hand from the water and jerked on the rope. A pale shape came toward me, breaking the surface with a plop of bubbles — snakes. It looked like a ganglion of white worms trailing from the neck, blood vessels, and a headless corpse.

| CHAPTER 18 |

I was on the porch about to enter the house when my aunt startled me by yanking the door open from the inside.

"A human head has turned up," she said. Quite matter of fact. "What next?"

"A head," I said. "We might have known."

"Perhaps not a head, actually. A skull would be more accurate. A very old one." The person who said this was a short man with wispy brown hair. He was sitting in my aunt's living room. He balanced a cup of tea on his knee; he held out the other hand and introduced himself to me: "Chalford. I'm the GP. Iron Falls. Do a bit of work for the coroner's office."

He gestured toward the chesterfield on which were seated two massive men in black raincoats and stout shoes. I had noticed a dark blue Crown Victoria parked in the drive. The smell of their leather shoes filled the front room, obliterating the potpourri that my aunt kept in a glass bowl on the mantel. There were introductions while Aunt Beth refilled the blue china teacups.

"You're the one supposed to have seen this body, out in the lagoon?" asked the first policeman. His name was Haggard. He seemed to be the one in charge. I nodded. I noticed no one was taking notes.

"Was it actually a corpse?" I asked.

"I don't know," said Detective Haggard. "What did you think it was?"

"Perhaps a tree."

"A tree?"

"Or a log."

"The report we heard was you'd seen a body."

"I guess I could have imagined it. Perhaps I was wrought up. You know, my father ..."

"Of course," Dr. Chalford interjected.

"As a boy, he had a very active imagination," said Aunt Beth.

"Floating free, was it?" said Haggard.

I told them that I'd been looking for the canoe, how I'd seen something tangled in the lines beneath an uprooted stump.

"Any idea who it might have been?" asked Haggard.

"J.D. Miller is the only person who has drowned around here in the past twenty years," I said.

"Not counting the Indian," said the other policeman.

"Miller," said Haggard. "There've been others round the lake, drowning. He's not the only one. And there could be some we don't know about. Suicides."

He slurped his tea. The cup looked tiny in his hand. "Good tea." He held out his cup for more. He seemed not about to ask more questions.

So I asked a question of Dr. Chalford. "How old do you think that body would be? I mean, just supposing, how long do you think it could have been there, in the lake?"

"To tell you the truth, I haven't the faintest idea."

"You think it has something to do with this boat, do you?" asked Haggard. The question was put to me.

"Maybe" I said.

"We know your dad was trying to pull the thing in. You've been asking around. Fellow at the marina told us."

"Your own investigation?" asked the other policeman.

"I'm not exactly investigating," I said.

"Neither are we," said Haggard. "We just have to fill out a report."

"What's this about finding a *head*?" I asked. I imagined it turning up in the water like a bobbing apple. But this was not the case.

"Skulls don't float. Some kid found it stuck in the mud out there, with the water so low. Ancient, like I say. Guess we'll send down to the lab in Toronto."

"Have you discovered anything else?" I asked.

"That you might be interested in? One thing: we think that old boat must have sunk on this side of the island, on the Merrick Bay side. No way could it have come around from the open lake. That was the idea, wasn't it? That the boat sank out in the rough water?"

They had done their homework. And I thought: Mrs. Applewood could have rammed the boat up on the cribs of the steamboat pier. She would have swum ashore and walked around the island to where we found her, sitting on the rocks, shivering. For her story.

"You want to know what I think?" Dr. Chalford said to me. "I doubt this *body* you say you've turned up was the old man, Miller, or at least, there's no possible way that we could ever tell. I think the body that you saw, granted you saw anything, had been trapped underwater — trapped for a very long time, no doubt — but twenty years? I don't know. I'm not an expert in this sort of thing, but I'll tell you roughly what happens to a body in water. The nails and hair, the skin and so on, all that starts to peel off. Fish eat the flesh."

"Sounds right," said Haggard.

"After a few months, the body fat turns into a waxy substance that more or less coats the bones and whatever's left of the organs. I believe that's what could have happened here. The body was trapped deep in cold water somewhere, by a tree, or by an old spar ..."

"Or in the cribbing of the old steamboat pier," I said.

"Perhaps. Something like that. Anyway, when the water was low this spring the thing breaks free, and washes into that old lagoon."

The same phenomenon that had brought the green rowboat to the surface. I had no idea until then that I had formed such a clear idea of what had happened.

"But the body I saw in the lagoon — there was no head. The head could have come off underwater, rubbing against the timbers of the cribbing, the thwarts of the boat."

"A certain grisly charm to that theory," said Dr. Chalford.

"Would that make it any more possible that it was this fellow Miller?" asked Detective Haggard.

"The head," said Dr. Chalford, "as I say, it's a skull really — seems to me more plausible that it could be the skull of this fellow who drowned, fell out of the boat or whatever it was, twenty-five years ago. A skull would last. And there's some sort of injury, up here —" he rapped the side of his own head twice with his knuckles "— which could have happened when he fell out of the boat. Could have hit himself on a rock or something."

"Could have been struck on the head," I said.

"Murder!" said the second policeman, smiling.

"On the other hand, he could have hit his head after he fell out of the boat, after he'd drowned," said Dr. Chalford. "I must tell you that postmortem injuries to bodies that are dragged from the water are common, extremely common. The bodies wash against rocks, they wash against piers, they get hit by boats and so on."

"So you can't identify either the body or the head, is that right?" I said. "Can't you get experts involved, dental records, that sort of thing?"

The police and Dr. Chalford looked at one another. "I suppose we could get experts involved," said Dr. Chalford. "I doubt if they'd be able to add much."

"Just so you know," said Haggard, looking at me and then at Dr. Chalford. "Before you both get carried away, there *is* no body to identify. Sent a man out to have a look in the lagoon this morning."

"Could have washed out to the lake again," said Dr. Chalford. He seemed rather excited. "Especially after Ray disturbed it, set it loose."

"I guess it could have," said Haggard.

"I thought you said it was a tree," said the other officer.

"Did they find anything?" I asked. "Anything at all?"

The policemen glanced at each other.

"Bit of old rope," said Haggard. "Kind you don't see anymore. Bit of old clothing around a spar. A few other bits and pieces." He slurped the last of his tea. "I suppose there could be something in what you're thinking. But we're not planning on doing anything more about it. That doesn't ruin your plans, does it? You go right ahead looking into it if you want. But the matter is closed as far as we're concerned."

"Closed?" I asked.

They thanked my aunt for the tea and left the house with a maximum of clumping and shuffling.

Dr. Chalford stayed a few minutes longer. He knew my aunt from social events in Iron Falls, and they chatted. Then I accompanied him to the door. On the porch, I asked him about snake bites. Garter snakes weren't even supposed to be toxic.

"But they can be," said Dr. Chalford. "Any snake bite can be toxic. And that number of bites in that short a time on someone so small. Certainly toxic. But don't ask. All that was long before my time."

| CHAPTER 19 |

Phil Havelock pointed to the bay, sparkling in the morning light. The exposed lake bottom had begun to dry — it appeared less otherworldly, almost benign — but the water had stopped falling and was beginning, almost imperceptibly, to rise again. Whatever mysteries or treasures the lake had given up would have to be claimed soon.

"I think the damn boat had been out there a few days by the time your dad came along, maybe longer," said Phil.

His son Kevin nodded in agreement. "I saw them gunwales sticking out of the water a few weeks back. Like old boards. Something out there, anyways. Didn't know what."

The three of us stood on the oily pier at the foot of River Street.

"We had some strong wind out of the northeast," said Phil, "You know how it blows in spring in these parts. The water kept going down — they still had all the dams and rivers wide open. Pretty soon you could actually see an old boat out there." He spat into the cattails.

"Lots of other stuff been turning," said Kevin. "I got some tires off of a '32 Ford."

"Someone else got a pump organ," said Phil. "Lots of planks from boats, oars and life jackets, stuff like that. Bras for some reason — teenagers, I guess. Couple of outboard motors. So who'd think anything of an old rowboat? No one but your dad."

"Even the Providence Island rowboat?" I asked. "Didn't people wonder about that?"

"Who could tell where the boat was from? Couldn't even tell the colour. Tell you the truth, Ray, we all pretty much forgot about that old rowboat, that whole story. Not until that corpse or whatever turned up in the lagoon last week. Set everybody to thinking. Ray's dead Indian, from the lagoon. Still, more than twenty years ago. Long time."

He slapped his coveralls, a way of ending the conversation. "Guess you came to see the damn thing. Kevin will show you. Come over to the garage after you're done, I'll get hold of that boy you wanted to talk to."

A half-century before, boats had been built at Merrick Bay: mahogany launches and sleek racing boats. Now the marina was an outlet for plastic hulls and Japanese motors; they were stacked out of doors in high, half-open sheds. The older wooden boats were stored in the boathouse, where they used to build them. I followed Kevin up the narrow wooden steps. We threaded our way in semi-darkness through the boats — monsters on sawhorses, shrouded in canvas — to the front of the room. Kevin leaned into a large wooden door and slid it open, letting daylight in. The green boat, which had been winched up onto a pallet, was directly in front of us. The muddy bay stretched below.

What was amazing was that so much of the boat remained intact. It had originally been a disappearing propeller boat, a skiff with a small engine in the centre. The propeller had fitted into a metal housing behind the engine into which it could be raised to pass through shallow water. There was no neutral or reverse, and the engine was infernally temperamental, Phil told me. It was usually in pieces on the worktable in the boathouse at the island, until they decided to remove the motor and the propeller altogether. The gunwales and some of the ribs were rotted through and crumbling, even the keel in places, but the curved planking of the sides remained nailed together and solid. Before being painted, the planks had been varnished for many years, and Kevin said that they would have remained largely impermeable to water.

"Not as bad as I expected," I said. "It would almost be possible to restore this boat."

"Rebuild is more like it. Cost a fortune," Kevin said. "Main trouble is with the keel, right in the middle here, where the motor used to be. The bottom would get spongy and waterlogged. This thing was heavy in the first place. Would have been hard to manoeuvre as a rowboat. And the decking is completely shot, you can see that. A lot of the ribbing, too."

"What about the hole?" I pointed to a gaping tear in the bottom, about a foot from the bow, just to the left of the keel.

"Have to replace the planking, is all," said Kevin.

"What happened there?"

"Looks like they slammed full tilt into a rock, a spar maybe, a spike, something. Water came rushing in, and the boat sank. Some guy drowned, right? Some old guy out with his nursemaid? Something like that. Stay and look around if you want to. I got to get back to work. You mind sliding that door shut when you're finished?"

I stared at the boat, hoping it would tell me something. I imagined myself in my father's shoes at the shore, staring out at the waves lapping at the gunwales, seized by a need to walk through the dead cattails and icy water.

I slid the big door shut. Mice scurried in the rafters.

"What were you hoping to find up there?" Phil asked, back in the office of the Merrick Hotel garage.

"Don't know, really. I'm trying to figure out why my father would be so worked up about an old boat. You said it had been out there for days. Nobody else seemed to care. Why should he?"

The door to the garage opened. A boy of about fourteen entered. He wore thick, wire-rimmed glasses, dark hair falling into his eyes. The boy from the hotel who had been with my father when he died.

My father had been grunting a lot as they pulled the boat up, the boy said. He'd had to stop and rest several times. When they reached the shore, my father's breathing became raspy.

"He was really white, and he was sweating across his forehead. I asked him if he was okay, and he sort of nodded. He took this hanky out of his pocket, and then he sits down in the grass, real sudden. Begins to wipe his forehead. Then he just keels over — face into the grass. I grabbed his shoulder. He didn't move. Then I rolled his head over so his mouth wouldn't be in the dirt. His lips were blue. His eyes were half-open. That's when I took off for the hotel."

Dr. Chalford had already told me that my father had died of a heart attack brought on by congestive heart failure.

The office of the Merrick Hotel garage was silent for a moment after these details of my father's death. Then I asked the boy about the boat, about how he had first seen my father out in the bay, pulling at something, looking as though he needed help.

"I saw him standing there pointing, like maybe he seen something besides that boat, I don't know what. When I got out there, he was trying to see if he could move it or something," the boy said. "He didn't want to pull it out at first. He said maybe we should just leave it there, you know, maybe the water would cover it up again. Then he looked out toward the lake. It didn't look like the water was going come back any time soon. The top of the boat was already starting to dry out a little. So we started dragging it toward shore."

"What did he want to do then?" I asked.

"He wanted to pull it up on the grass and set it on fire."

"Right then and there?"

"It was soaking wet. That's how come it was so heavy. We were going to put it in some bushes there, let it dry out. Be dry in a day or two, that's what he said. Then we'd come back, break it up, and drag the pieces onto the beach."

"The beach?"

"Would've made some awesome fire."

After the boy had left, I asked Phil, "What do you think happened to that boat?"

"You mean, last week, or more than twenty years ago?"

"Twenty-three years ago."

"They rowed around the island, the wind came up, the boat sank. I don't know. It's happened before. It'll happen again. Last year, couple of kids killed themselves driving a big Donzi up on the rocks out here. That's the way it is. You're just interested in this rowboat because the Millers are involved."

"What do people around here think?"

"They don't think about it much. Some of the old ones — my mother and her friends — they used to make up stories: maybe she pushed him over. Years ago she was supposed to have had an affair with him."

"Who?"

"Mrs. Applewood, when she was a girl. It's just a story. But that's what they used to do, these summer people. Come up here and look for local talent. You know they got table dancing down at the Shalomar now? Christ, the things they get up to, about six inches from your face."

"Have you seen Marjorie Applewood?" I asked.

"I haven't seen old Marj in twenty years. She came back from St. Thomas, but she never came back from Galt. Moved down there with some cousin. Her mother was already going strange. Began when her old man died. Old Marj, she used to write poetry and stuff, did you know that? All about death. Put it in the school magazine. So she finished school down in Galt, went off to university somewhere down east. Don't know where she is now. You ought to ask Donny. He's living out behind the old place somewhere. Hardly ever comes into town."

As we spoke, he had been sweeping out the office, the mid-morning lull in business. He stopped now, holding the broom in front of him.

"You remember that time at the picnic ground?" he said.

"Not much," I said, "what about it?"

"Just wondering — about old Marj." Phil said. "Yeah, I guess the best thing is not to remember too much, eh? You been reading the papers lately? Because I guess what went on that night, I guess nowadays that'd be called some kind of *assault* and LaTroppe and a few of the boys, they'd maybe have gone to jail."

A car pulled up at the pumps. Phil leaned the broom against the counter and left me in the office. There was a Pirelli calendar on the wall, another from the local real estate company beside it. There were piles of greasy yellow invoices on the counter, and pink phone messages and memos jammed on a silver spike. There was a pile of unopened envelopes, today's mail. One of these was a small rectangular package, about the size of an ordinary envelope, but much thicker and wrapped in protective paper. The address was in purple ink, and it was written in a small, squarish hand that was familiar to me. I picked the package up to examine the writing more closely.

"See anything you like there, Ray?" Phil sauntered back into the office. He had a credit card in his hand.

"Oh, just looking at this package, the writing …"

"Right. From an old friend of yours." I looked up. He slipped the credit card and a blank invoice into the imprinter.

"What's this all about," I asked.

"All's I know is you better put that thing back on the desk, behind the counter there," Phil said, pointing. Then he winked. "We don't want any other town councillors and such to see it, do we?"

He slammed the imprinter across the credit card and returned to his customer. I put the package back on the desk, but not before glancing at it again. The parcel had been mailed in Iron Falls two days before. The same small letters, the same purple ink: I hadn't seen them in twenty years. Quentin's handwriting.

| CHAPTER 20 |

I returned to see Phil two days later. I wanted to look at the envelope and her handwriting one more time. Phil wouldn't show me. He wouldn't say why. I imagined he was ashamed of his corruption, whatever it was, ashamed of what I might learn. The people of Merrick Bay liked to project an image of country virtue. Plain folk. Honest folk.

"It's not my business," I said. "I'm sorry I looked at it. Can I see it just for a minute?"

Phil stood behind the counter, head down, filling out some form. After half a minute, he glanced up. "It's really not much. I'm not the only one, that's for sure."

"Doesn't matter," I said.

"Whether I'm in or not, it's going through. Everything around here does, sooner or later."

"I don't care," I said. "I don't care about any of that. Neither does anyone else." I only cared about the purple ink, the small handwriting.

"The big house will come down," Phil said. "The guest houses are already sold. They'll keep the boathouses, use one as a cottage and sell the others. The property will be divided into lots. The island's about twenty-five acres. Comes out to about ten good-sized lots. Nothing wrong with that, right?"

"Nothing," I said. "The Millers still greasing palms? Big Deal."

But he wouldn't give me the package.

"Why won't you let me see it?" I asked.

"What if someone asks questions, asks you what you know?"

"I never saw anything."

"What you said — greasing palms. What kind of talk is that? What if someone heard you? A customer?"

"I will never mention their name again," I said. "Can I see it?"

"I don't have it. I took it to the bank."

This was a lie. It was nine o'clock Monday morning; he'd had the package on Friday afternoon. There was a look on his face.

"All right, don't show it to me," I said. "Just take a look. Tell me where it was mailed. If there's a return address."

He stared for a moment, then said, "Wait here."

I heard him rummaging in the back office, the spinning and click of a combination lock. In the window of the door between the two offices I saw his reflection. He was examining the package. I was sorry he had to hide from me. He returned the package to the safe and slammed the door shut.

"No return address," he said. "The package was mailed in Iron Falls, though, which is odd."

"Why is that odd?"

"They usually send about five hundred U.S. in fifties. Not by mail. From somewhere in Pennsylvania by courier. Why are you so interested?"

"The address. It's in Quentin Miller's handwriting. She must be in the area."

"I heard she was around here a few weeks back. If she's in Iron Falls, there are only two places someone like her would stay. Holiday Inn or the River House." He shook his head. "You and that woman."

"She's a spinster," Aunt Beth said. "A *university professor*."

"A couple of things I want to ask her, that's all," I said.

My aunt put down her knitting. "About the boat, I suppose."

"Do you ever see Mrs. Applewood?" I asked.

"Poor old Mrs. Applewood." This was how she referred to her, even though Mrs. Applewood was at least ten years younger than my aunt. "First it was the nervous breakdown. Now she's losing her marbles. They put her away — the old ski place down the highway that they've turned into a nursing home."

"I'd like to speak to Donny, too."

"That old house. I don't see how anyone could possibly live out there."

"And I need to ask Quentin about that time my father came up to J.D. You remember that golf game? Do you know why he came to see the old man? What they talked about?"

"I have no idea. He never discussed his business with me. What difference could it make now? All those years. I can't believe that's the reason that you're going to Iron Falls."

"What difference does it make?" I said, echoing her.

"Why are you so interested?" she asked. "It was fate. He was old. It was his time to go."

I didn't ask whether she meant J.D. or my father.

There was no Quentin Miller (I assumed that that was the name she would be going by) at the Holiday Inn. I tried the River House.

"We have a Dr. Miller staying here," said the man at the desk.

"Dr. Miller?" I asked.

"Not a real doctor. Some kind of professor. Shall I put you through?"

I said no. Something made me think that if I asked her, just phoned up to her room, Quentin wouldn't agree to see me.

"Is she alone?" I asked. A big city hotel wouldn't have answered, but he did. Quentin was alone.

I thanked him and hung up the phone. I would drop in on her later that day, see her before dinner, and ask her for a drink in the lobby.

Dusk. As I drove the twelve miles from Merrick Bay to Iron Falls, the farmland fell into shadows. The dark forests seemed to be marching down the hills from the north. Closer to town, the reflections of the lights from houses and street lamps rippled in the surface of the river. The River House was Iron Falls' most exclusive hotel; not the biggest, which was the Holiday Inn, or the newest, which was the Slumberland, but the most up-market, with pretensions to a country inn. It stood high on a hill overlooking the falls. I turned off the engine. I'd been in Merrick Bay for a week. I gazed at the lights along the river, the edge of new development and the blackness of the forests beyond. I remembered lights from a hotel window, the last time I'd seen Quentin Miller.

I was in New York for academic meetings, a convention for universities and people looking for teaching positions. Representatives from colleges all over the continent were there to talk to people who were in their last year of graduate school. I was testing the waters; this was before I dropped out of MIT for the last time and moved west. I'd been in New York several times during my time in Boston, but always with others. After recovering from evenings in bars and nightclubs, we would browse in bookstores and galleries. We stayed on the floors of friends' places in Brooklyn and Queens. I'd never looked up Quentin then.

But this time I was alone. I was staying at the Sheraton on Seventh Avenue. I reached her through the Morgan Library. She no longer worked there, but she still came in from time to time. They had her address. Somewhere in the East Village. They gave me a telephone number.

"This is a surprise," she said when I reached her. I'd been hoping for something more. I suggested we get together for a drink.

"I could pick up a bottle of wine, bring it over to your place," I said. I had imagined that we then might go out for dinner somewhere and then to some club.

"My place?" she said. "I don't think so. Where are you staying?"

I told her. She said she would be at my room at about six o'clock.

I spent the afternoon wandering through the hospitably suites and booths of universities. There were elaborate lists of positions available. It was still early in the meetings; time for discussions rather than formal interviews, the first of which would begin the following day. I made no arrangements for appointments. I returned to my room early to rest and shower. I changed into dark pants and a blazer. I strolled west a couple of blocks to a liquor store where I bought a bottle of wine from the cooler. At a delicatessen I purchased smoked salmon, cream cheese, tiny fresh bagels. The sidewalks grew crowded as offices emptied. A prostitute sidled up beside me. "Hi, handsome. Want a date?" I brushed my way past her into the hotel.

Quentin was half an hour late. I opened the door and she stood there in the hall, wearing blue jeans, a faded ribbed turtleneck, a light raincoat. I felt foolish in my jacket and tie.

We did not rush into each other's arms. We did not kiss. We did not embrace.

"Sorry I'm late," Quentin said.

I showed her in, took her coat. I put the bottle of cold wine on the table beside a couple of glasses.

"You mind if I take a little something first?" she asked.

"I don't mind."

She sat down at the desk and took from her purse an envelope and a small mirror. She poured the powder from the envelope onto the mirror. She made a tube out of a dollar bill and snorted. She offered the tube to me.

"No thanks," I said. She shrugged. "All right, I'll try it." I took as little as possible. "You do this a lot?"

"It relaxes me," she said.

I opened the wine and poured us each a glass. I unwrapped the salmon and cream cheese and put them on the table beside the bread.

"Are you still playing tennis?" she asked. It was a long time since I had seen her. Was tennis all that there was to talk about? I told her what I knew about the people in Merrick Bay, what I'd learned in phone calls and letters and in my visits back to Toronto, about all the silent men who had died (Mr. Ault, Mr. Havelock, the man at the marina) while the women remained, about Donny Applewood becoming some kind of hermit, about Phil becoming a master mechanic and getting married, about Chicklet — Jerry Reed — how he had left Merrick Bay and become a sportscaster in Barrie.

"Who are these people?" asked Quentin. "Who on earth is Chicklet?"

She leaned back against the chesterfield, smoking a cigarette, gently moving her legs apart and together again. I sat across from her on the end of the bed. I stood up. Through the window, I saw the lights of Manhattan sparkling in the blue night. I leaned forward and kissed her on the lips. They tasted salty and electric. She didn't put her arms around me.

"Ray, how cruel of you. For old times' sake — that's why I thought you wanted to see me. When all you wanted was to get drunk and fuck me." She looked around the room. "This is an awful hotel. I don't believe I've ever been here before."

The drug made it difficult to read her. My nose and lips felt frozen, as though I were anaesthetized.

I asked her about Jack. She didn't answer; she was in some kind of reverie. Then she said, "He's fine. He finished Harvard Law." She leaned back, took a sip of wine, and puffed her cigarette. "You remember that time in the pump house?" It was as though she were reading my mind. But then she said, "What about that girl Marjorie? You ever talk to Jack about that? Christ, what a mess that was."

"What?" I asked. "What did you say?"

She turned and looked at me. "I said — Christ. Nothing, Ray. Nothing."

The drug must have affected me more than I knew. I felt a wave of relief. It was a vision, a fear I'd had ever since those dreams of snakes when the stories first began to circulate. We dream every night, but only some of the dreams have meaning. The vocabulary of dreams is supposed to be universal. Snakes. I realized that I had of course thought that the child was perhaps Quentin's and mine.

"What about dinner?"

"Actually, I'm on my way somewhere. Meeting a friend. I'm sorry, Ray — you were expecting to make an evening of it." She reached out and touched my wrist. Her fingers were cool on my skin. "Call me if you're in town again."

"I'll see you out."

"No need."

But I was already on my feet, fumbling at the door. When we reached the elevator, I accompanied her down to the lobby and then to the street.

"Are you seeing me out, or following me?" Quentin asked. But I needed the fresh air. The wine was sour in my throat.

We crossed the sidewalk to the curb. I flagged a taxi. I held the door, and at last she turned and kissed me, one hand around my neck.

"Have a nice life," she said. I closed the car door and watched the taxi merge into the traffic. Someone tapped me on my shoulder. I turned.

"Hiya, handsome." It was the same hooker.

"I bet you say that to all the boys," I said.

"Only the good-looking ones."

"Your timing is perfect."

"What do you expect? I'm a pro."

She put her arm through mine. The height of the heels she wore made her wobble, but no one in the lobby turned as we walked through. Upstairs, the room stank of fish. The cold salmon curled on the table.

"Got no Mrs. Miller staying here. No Dr. Miller. No Professor Miller, either."

The man at the front desk of the River House didn't look up from his computer screen as he told me this.

"But I phoned earlier."

"Yeah? Well, she checked out. This morning, it looks like here."

"You have her home address?"

"Can't give it out."

"Listen, I'm an old friend of hers. I know she teaches somewhere in Upstate New York. Elmira, Ithaca. Somewhere like that."

"Like I say, pal, I can't give it out."

But he finally did give me a forwarding address that she had left, a street in Toronto. It wasn't far from the house where I had lived as a boy.

| CHAPTER 21 |

She was still striking, her golden hair only a little dulled by time, her hazel-green eyes still arresting. Her appearance was looser than it had been when she was young; now she walked with a kind of stride. She had small lines across her forehead, and crow's feet. Her perfume, though: I thought that was the same.

"How did you find me?"

"You know I'll always find you, Quentin."

I'd intended this as mock-romantic, ironic and world-weary, but it came off as ominous. I was still pursuing. She was still oblivious.

I told her about what I'd discovered, the money being sent to Merrick Bay, the whisper of corruption. She rolled her eyes.

"Christ, it's all *so* stupid, sending money in the mail like that, but they've been doing it for years. My grandfather started it all. Now it's Jack, and some of my cousins. They can't stop. The funny thing is originally they *didn't* want any land sold up there. They wanted the councillors on side. Now, it's because they *do* want it sold."

"They?" I asked.

"All right, we. *We* can use the money. You don't have to be so sanctimonious about it."

She had spent several years in England, at Oxford, and now she spoke in a rather British way, turning up her sentences at the end, with a tendency to be clipped rather than languid.

She offered me a drink. She made herself a whisky and soda.

"You're married now, I suppose?" she said. "I always thought you were the marrying type."

She made it sound like some bank clerk, a scurrying little fellow with brown suits and squeaky shoes.

I told her about my divorce, about Katie.

"Are you married?" I asked.

"Not at the present time."

"Any prospects?"

"Not at the present time."

"But there have been in the past?"

"When I was living in New York. But then he invited me to an orgy. Salvador Dali was supposed to show up."

"What was it like?"

"It was disgusting. Like some nightmare locker room."

"What about Salvador Dali?"

"He never showed."

I told her about my stay in Merrick Bay. My visits to Phil Havelock and other people she might have known. She showed little interest and didn't recall any of them.

"You remember Jerry Reed — you and he and Phil Havelock, getting drunk on the trampoline," I said.

"I don't remember."

I told her about the pale, waxy torso that I thought I had seen in the water of the dark lagoon.

"The headless Indian," she said, mocking. "At last someone has seen him."

I alluded to the fact that I had thought it could have been her father.

"Yeah? What difference would it make?" she said. "That was a lifetime ago, and he was a self-centred old prick. He's been dead over twenty years. I don't give a shit."

She poured herself another glass of whisky.

"You know what people say," I said.

"Yes, I know what they say. That the nursemaid pushed him out. Hit him over the head with that cane and shoved him overboard. Something like that. Christ, I wouldn't blame her."

"Why not?"

"Years before — before he was married to my mother, and when that woman was only a girl herself — he had some kind of fling with her."

"Do you know this?"

"Family rumour. But I believe it. *Droit de seigneur*. It was a tradition among the men in our family. Fuck the locals — hey, if any of them were good-looking enough."

The telephone rang. She answered, and I heard her making arrangements for someone to drop by in about half an hour or so.

When she returned to the living room, she said, "Nice to see you and everything, Ray — all that. And I was sorry to hear about your father, saw it in the paper. But why are you still hanging around up there in Merrick Bay, talking to all these people? Why can't you leave it all alone? Go home to your wife or girlfriend, or whatever she is."

I couldn't go home, not yet. I had to answer the questions that had been raised by the surfacing of the green rowboat, and by my father's death.

"Or did you come back to see me?" asked Quentin.

"I can't believe you think that," I said.

"The price of being gorgeous and intelligent." She yawned.

"I'm trying to find out why my father died," I said.

"You just told me: he was closing in on seventy-five and he had a bad heart. What more do you want?"

"Before he died, just before, he walked out into the middle of Merrick Bay. He had spotted an old boat, the green rowboat from Providence Island. Did you know that?"

"How on earth would I know what your father was looking at when he died? Is this some sort of father-son thing? You hadn't yet come to peace with him? Please."

"Partly that," I said. "Partly the business of that boat, your father falling out of it."

"My father was a prick. Don't waste your time worrying about him."

"Your brother ..."

"My half-nephew, you mean. Another prick. All the men in my family are pricks."

"The baby," I said, for I understood at last that this was the heart of the matter.

"You mean my — whatever it was — baby," said Quentin.

"Your baby?"

"Isn't that what you meant?" asked Quentin. "I thought it was."

She looked away for a moment.

I remembered something that she had said to me in New York fifteen years before in my room at the Sheraton. She had said, *"You remember that time in the pump house? What if I'd been the one?"*

"You had a baby?" I asked.

"It was looked after," she said. "We looked after it."

I gazed at her, as if asking a question.

She looked back with her hard hazel eyes, and I had the old hallucinatory experience, seeing her in the green light of the forest in July, seeing her knife into the water, seeing her naked, seeing her run through the woods toward me the day her father drowned, seeing her pale skin in the darkness, her mouth, her lips.

"Looked after it?"

"Christ, the Millers, you idiot," she said. "We look after everything."

I stared at her.

"I thought J.D. might have told you something about it that day he went to meet you," she said, "the day we were supposed to play tennis."

"Me?" My face felt hot, flushed. "We only ..."

"That night. I know, Ray. You don't have to tell me. Remember? You were rather pathetic with your arm. Hadn't I made you climb that rock cliff? That was madness, doing that with a person like you. You should never have been up on the rocks like that."

"A person like me?"

"I didn't mean to insult you. It was the night Jack and his father had that godawful fight. They actually hit each other, did you know that? And then J.D. told Jack's father to fuck off and get out of the house."

I remembered that fight. Quentin and I were eating dinner alone on the side verandah.

"Why were they fighting?" I was reeling. Had I known?

"Some things I can't tell you, Ray. Or I shouldn't tell you. Won't tell you. You'll have to ask him yourself. Or ask Marjorie Applewood. A certain irony. A certain parallel. As an English teacher, I am, of course, aware of these things."

"I can't believe it," I said. "Just the one night."

"Just the one night in that stinking stone hut or whatever it was, but we must have done 'it,' as we used to say, four or five times. Maybe more. And as you know, it only takes one to do the job."

"You could have told me at the time …"

"Why? You didn't think we were going to get together and have a little Carrier, did you? Me? Jesus, I mean, a roll in the hay's one thing …"

She leaned forward and began rummaging around in her bag for a pack of cigarettes.

"When I think — all the trouble, all the business with boys and sex and all those close calls, was my period going to come or wasn't it, abortions — I've had three, by the way, so you don't have to get yourself into some kind of moral dilemma. The sex in particular: overrated. Apart from French kissing, I never really enjoyed the whole business. Not just with you, Ray, with anyone. The whole thing is just too much damn trouble." She lit a cigarette, took a languid draw. She was either bored or affecting it; I couldn't tell. "All these things — I mean morality and sex — you talk about then in the abstract, but they never happen in the abstract. It's always a meeting of two people, individuals, a coming together, if you'll pardon the expression. And then they have to decide what to do. Or at least, one of them does. Usually the woman, in my experience. When people have sex, Ray, they get pregnant. Quite often, that's what happens. I seem to be at risk of giving a lecture here. And you seem to be at risk of becoming sanctimonious. Perhaps it would be better if you left?"

I didn't care about her lecture. I thought that Quentin didn't care a hoot about individuals.

"Goodbye, Ray," she said. She held the door open for me.

"We're always saying goodbye," I said.

"Somehow I have the feeling this will be the last time," she said.

The night was warm, almost muggy. From her house I walked to a lounge that we used to sneak into when I was a teenager, the only one in the neighbourhood. The place had become a strip joint. I sat at the bar and had three shots of whisky. A naked woman wrapped herself around the brass pole. I ordered a beer. When I returned to my hotel, I was drunk.

| CHAPTER 22 |

I had returned to Merrick Bay from my overnight in Toronto. Several days had passed since the funeral, a time that many might view as a period of quiet mourning, when Aunt Beth asked me, "Well, what are you going to do with yourself today? Surely not another day in the house?"

"I thought you might like the company. I thought you might be lonely without my father."

"I appreciate your concern. But you must understand, before I came here, I lived by myself for thirty years. When your father was here, he was either in his study or in the garden. And he was often out."

"Where?"

"Walking. He sometimes drove to the city. Or visiting people in the district."

"Who?"

"All sorts of people. I don't know who. Mrs. Applewood, down at Lake Park Lodge, for one."

"Mrs. Applewood?"

"He liked to keep in touch, to see how she was doing. You know he kept a few clients after he retired, local people who were glad not to have to drive to Iron Falls to see a lawyer. She was one of them."

Season in and season out the windows in the corridors and in the lounges and bedrooms were sealed shut. People who all their lives had lived close to the smells and sounds of this particular bit of countryside — in the spring, wind-borne yellow pine dust; in the summer, breezes from the lakes and the ripple of aspen leaves — were now sealed inside a kind of stale motel; the odour was that mix of bedding and perfumed disinfectant that travellers know, or even worse: wafts of kitchen scents, old cafeteria, the smell of sickness.

In the late afternoon it was hard to see through the grime of the window, to see the pine forest that rose on the hill behind the building, and the bright lights turned the glass to mirrors. Gentle music came over the PA system.

I followed one of the attendants, a matronly woman in rumpled white, along the corridor. "Here we are, sweetie," she said brightly. "Dinnertime in half an hour."

It was a double room, with both beds neatly made up. There were built-in drawers, bedside tables covered with family photographs, and at the foot of each bed a small armchair. Mrs. Applewood sat in one of these.

When I had last seen her, she had been a slight woman; now she was immense. Even her face seemed to have grown large and round, from drugs, I supposed. Her diagnosis was unclear. I had spoken with the director of Lake Park Lodge — she had warmed considerably on hearing that I was Mr. Carrier's son — and she had told me that Alzheimer's could only be definitively diagnosed after death. Mrs. Applewood wasn't as bad as some, she said. True, she often became disoriented, and before she came into the lodge she used to wander; several times Donny found her as far away as the highway. She was excitable, prone to bursts of sudden emotion, laughter or tears. She sometimes swore. And although she could feed herself, the problem was how to make sure she didn't eat too much, not too little. "Just shovels it in like there's no tomorrow," the director said. She was as a rule not incontinent, she could converse and enjoy jokes, and there were periods where she seemed able to remember much, especially from the distant past. Perhaps there had been a small stroke. Perhaps there had been some other illness or traumatic event, a fall, some long-forgotten childhood accident. "Would you know of any such incident? Or accident? A fall, perhaps?"

I said I knew of nothing. (It was not particularly something I wanted to go into.)

Mrs. Applewood turned when I entered the room. She was well groomed, and she had always had a lovely smile. As a young woman, she had been a famous beauty in Merrick Bay, and there was still something of that about her.

"I know it smells bad in here. I don't even notice it," she said. "Who the hell are you?"

"Ray Carrier."

"Phil Havelock's friend." She said it instantly, triumphantly. "Nice boy. Neighbours of ours, you know. The Havelocks. Oh, yes. The mother talked all the time. Talk, talk, talk. Nice little woman, though. The husband — what's his name — he was a drunk."

"And John Carrier's son."

"John? What was that?"

"My father was John Carrier. He was your lawyer."

"My lawyer. Isn't that wonderful? Marvellous. My lawyer. Oh, yes, he was a great help."

When she was drifting, her face took on a placid expression, like a smooth and shiny mask.

"How is Marjorie?" I asked.

"Marjorie." She brightened. "Oh, yes. Marjorie. She's fine. Just fine. Marvellous."

I rose from my chair and walked to the bedside table. There were several photos of Marjorie. There were pictures of a couple of children, as babies and as teenagers. Marjorie's children, I supposed. There was a photo of Donny, looking not so very different from how I remembered him. There was a faded picture of Mr. Applewood standing in front of the barn, smiling and squinting into the camera. I had never met Mr. Applewood, but he looked friendly and garrulous — where Marjorie must have gotten her nature.

And, in a black wooden frame behind the others, there was a copy of the picture of my father, Mrs. Applewood, and John D. Miller in front of the 1942 Packard, the autumn day of the famous golf game.

I remembered that day. It was in the fall, the summer after I'd met the Millers. My summer with Quentin.

"I won't be home until dinner," my father had said. He hadn't looked up from his paper. His tone and expression were, as usual, opaque.

"Won't be home till dinner?" Aunt Beth had asked. In the city, she came to us for Friday dinners. "Where on earth are you going?"

"Merrick Bay."

"Merrick Bay?" my aunt and I spoke almost in the same breath. "At this time of year? What on earth for?" she asked. "The house isn't open. The rat poison's out." She paused, letting this sink in, the risk that the trip posed to my father's very life. Then she said, "It's not business, is it?"

He occasionally drove to Merrick Bay in the winter to see some of the people for whom he did a little work there, real estate and wills mostly, but he had never before gone on a Saturday.

"Business? In a way, yes," my father said.

"Rather mysterious," said my aunt.

"He's going to play golf!" I said. I had seen his clubs outside the back door. And so he had to admit it: he was driving up to play golf. With J.D. Miller.

My father hadn't played golf since my mother's death; he had never actually liked the game in the first place; he didn't like games of any kind. And after all his denunciations of people like the Millers (and the Millers in particular) my aunt and I were astounded. I had wondered at the time how J.D. could play golf: since his last stroke, two years before, he could hardly walk, though he was improving. My father said that it seemed he could swing the club once he had been helped to the ball. Of course, they would have a cart, and a caddy. (It must have been the caddy that took the photograph, one copy of which now sat on the bureau in my aunt's guest room and another on Mrs. Applewood's bedside table at Lake Park Lodge. I wondered why the photos were kept. A memento of my father and his victory, perhaps.) And it wouldn't matter how slow they were because they would be the only ones on the course; the club had officially closed. But if J.D. wanted to play, they opened up, and that was what the club was doing on this occasion.

When he'd arrived home that evening, my father went straight to the pantry — built-in cabinets with mullioned doors, gumwood trim — and poured himself a couple of fingers of rye straight from the bottle into a kitchen glass. No ice. No trip to the crystal decanter in the dining room from which he usually poured his drink.

"How was your game?" I asked.

"Fine."

"Did you beat him?"

"No."

And that was all that was ever said about it. Ever. It was the last game of golf that either my father or J.D. played. The photograph turned up years later. Somebody, either Marjorie or Donny or one of the relations (my aunt wasn't sure who), sent it over when they were clearing out Mrs. Applewood's things, getting ready for her move into the home.

I was surprised again at how lives intersected. I supposed that she had kept this photo to remind her of that. Or perhaps it was something else — her triumph as much as my father's. She was still remarkable-looking in the photo; you could see in her face the pretty girl she must have been at eighteen, her eyes especially. Perhaps she wanted to remind herself of that, of what her life had been, and the direction that it might have taken.

I held the photo up so that Mrs. Applewood could see it. Her face became animated again.

"Oh, yes. They used to go dancing. Across the lake in the big motorboat to the dance hall! One time Louis Armstrong was there." She clapped her hands. "Satchmo!"

"Who used to go dancing?" I asked her.

"The girl. The beautiful young girl in the picture. Brown hair. She had such lovely brown hair!" She made a cascading gesture in front of her to demonstrate the hair. Then she carefully folded her hands in front of her. The smooth look came to her face. I tried to bring her back.

"Mrs. Applewood, I wanted to ask you about Mr. Miller. Old Mr. Miller. J.D. You used to look after him. You remember — he fell out of the green rowboat."

"The garbage boat! That goddamn fucking boat! Oh — excuse my French."

"Yes, the garbage boat. You used to row him around the island in that boat."

"Around the island?" She turned and looked out the window. I gazed at her reflection. She was suddenly puzzled. What pictures were flashing through her mind? She turned to me and said. "The canoe, you mean. Or was it the rowboat? Were you the boy in the canoe? The boy on the river?"

"The rowboat, Mrs. Applewood. Mr. Miller fell out of the green rowboat, the boat that used to be the Providence Island garbage boat. He fell out of the boat and drowned."

"Disappeared!"

"That's right, Mrs. Applewood. Disappeared."

"He was a cripple! That horrible black cane. He couldn't swim at all! Of course he drowned! I can just see him there, standing straight up on the bottom of the lake, drownded." She realized she had mispronounced the word and tried again. "Drowned, like. And do you know the funny thing?"

"What?"

"The reason they came here in the first place, the Millers, they didn't like the *ocean*. They didn't want all that water around. That's why they came up here to these lakes. *Our* lakes. And then that old man drowns! Ha!" She rocked forward and slapped her knee.

"What happened? Did you run into the cribs, the old steamboat pier?"

"Oh, I don't know what happened. Don't know." She turned to the window again. "The beautiful girl. The beautiful young girl." She was almost whispering.

"Mrs. Applewood? Mrs. Applewood?" I touched her arm. She looked around. Her face was blank. Her head fell back on the chair, exhausted. I would learn nothing more here.

A young woman in a green uniform stuck her head in the open doorway. "Hi, honey. Suppertime." And then to me, "You're welcome to come along down. She'd like that." She turned to Mrs. Applewood "Wouldn't you, sweetie." And then again to me, "You can feed her, if you want."

I took Mrs. Applewood's arm and accompanied her down to what was a combined lounge and dining area at the end of the hall. About eight tables had been set. Some of the old people were in wheelchairs. Apparently those who could or who wanted to ate in the main cafeteria; the others ate in the lounges similar to this one located on each floor.

The attendant helped Mrs. Applewood with her napkin, tucking it inside the collar of her dress like a bib. Mrs. Applewood dealt with the tomato juice in three noisy gulps. A television babbled in the corner.

"Mrs. Applewood, where is Marjorie?" I asked. But by then she was concentrating on her food, slathering the butter in great yellow swaths on her bread, her mashed potatoes, the brightly coloured peas and corn niblets, and she didn't hear me. The smell of that place was suddenly overwhelming, and I fled.

On the way out, I asked for Marjorie Applewood's address and phone number from the Lake Park Lodge office.

"Are you a doctor?" the woman asked. "Are you family? We're not supposed to give that information out. Rules. You might try that brother, though. Everyone around here knows where he lives."

"Where?" I asked.

"Back in the country. The old Allen place. Out past Merrick Centre."

The haunted house. Donny lived in the haunted house.

| CHAPTER 23 |

The Havelocks' farm: abandoned. The Applewoods' farm on Sucker Creek: abandoned. The Applewoods' other farmhouse — where the hired hand used to stay; three small rooms downstairs, three small rooms upstairs; never painted on the outside, so the wood had turned dark; children used to call it the black house and were afraid to go near it, made monsters of whatever poor drifter or foreigner ("new Canadians," they were called) Mr. Applewood might have staying there — the black house: that, too, was now abandoned.

This was the house into which Mrs. Applewood and Donny had moved the year after Mr. Applewood was killed by the falling willow, the year poor Mrs. Applewood stopped being cultivated, stopped being known for putting on airs, and started being known for getting a little queer, a little strange, something not quite right in the head. The truth was the people of Merrick Bay preferred her that way. They sympathized. They understood going a little queer in the head after seeing your husband crushed to death beneath a tree better than they understood putting on airs because you had been pretty as a girl and had a little education.

The black house tilted so much it looked drunk; it was difficult to understand how it still stood, how it could endure even a gentle wind, if ever wind came into this shallow valley.

"It's hard to believe there is anyone left to come to your meetings," I said to my aunt, driving past the empty house. "Where did they all go?"

Close to the lake, the roads in summer were choked with traffic. Weekend boating now made swimming in Merrick Bay virtually impossible. There was creeping strip development. After the beginning of August, people were advised not to drink the lake water because of E.coli: seepage from people's septic tanks, so it was said. Development along and immediately behind the lake was becoming denser and denser every year; some real estate agents were even hungrily starting to call Merrick Bay "an all season resort community."

And yet here, just a couple of miles back, what had once been farm country, the land was becoming emptier and emptier. The roads through the country behind the lakes were dotted with abandoned houses, collapsing barns, derelict sheds and chicken coops, and in the fields — what fields there were between the stands of forest and granite outcrops — rusting ploughs and harrows, the relentless march of weedy trees, saplings sprouting where once there had been pasturage for cows and sheep.

"The children leave. The old people die," Aunt Beth said. "That's the story of life, actually."

Stoic and matter-of-fact. How different she was from my mother, who had been flighty, nervous, given even as an adult to blushing and sudden hysterical laughter. Aunt Beth and my father were in many ways a better match; it should not have surprised me as much as did that over the years, those summers and more recently, that they had lived under the same roof for longer than my father and mother had ever been married.

Aunt Beth rolled the window down an inch or two. The interior of the car smelled of hot plastic. Morning in mid-June, a warm day, and already the countryside looked like high summer. Except for that new sheen of green to everything. This greenness: it was a look we never got in Idaho.

I was taking my aunt to the meeting of the Women's Institute. It was a long drive, all the way to the next township; several local branches had amalgamated in response to declining membership. The young generation in the organization were now women of sixty. But my aunt wasn't concerned that the WI might wither and die. That was just the way of things.

After I dropped her off at the community centre in which the meeting was to be held — the building sat curiously alone at the side of the road, no other sign of human habitation within sight — I doubled partway back along the road we had come.

The Allen place. We used to call it the haunted house. *Don't go near it,* my parents would warn me, amazed at how far eleven-year-olds could travel on their bicycles, how far up the creek we could get in the green punt or on our homemade rafts or in the yellow canoe. The barn might fall down, they said. The floors might be rotten. There might be abandoned wells — you would fall deep into the darkness and never get out. There was dangerous old machinery, rusty barbed-wire fences. And strangers. Strangers sometimes went there. Tramps from the freight trains. People who went there to drink. They threw bottles through the windows and shat on the floors. On the trampled grass outside the Allen house, next to an old mattress someone had dragged outside, I examined the first condom I had ever seen. "For protection from disease only" were the words printed on it.

The Allen house was one of the places where Bert was supposed to have stayed when he was in the area, those years when he was on the lam from the police, another of our ghosts. Motorcycle gangs went there. Drifters. Low women and "white trash," as Mrs. Havelock remarked. And now Donny Applewood, moving deeper and deeper into the countryside, lived at the Allen place; he had gotten it for next to nothing and somehow made it habitable.

I drove by the entrance on the first pass. The front field was completely grown over so that the house, a quarter of a mile back from the road, was hidden from view. An iron gate hung permanently half-open, its lower end embedded in baked mud. The driveway — two deep ruts with a hump of high weeds in the middle — curved around the gate, then followed a gentler curve between two rows of dead elms to the farmyard.

In the high grass all round were the skeletal hulks of wrecked cars and trucks. There were small piles of tires, doors, fenders, bumpers, and other parts. In the midst of all this, an old stove and fridge. The inevitable dogs prowled the hard-packed dirt directly in front of the house, but these dogs were less fearsome than fearful. They reminded me of the craven half-dead dogs you saw in Mexico, or in the poor villages of the Caribbean, the interior of places like St. Lucia.

The house was faded white with robin's egg blue trim. One of the two windows on either side of the front door was covered with blotchy cardboard. The front door was shut, a dirty curtain across the window. There was no sign of life, and the approach to the house, though overgrown with raspberry bushes, was somehow foreboding. I stepped from the car and slammed the door shut. I was enveloped in the silence of the countryside. The only sound was the drone of insects.

I called out. "Hello? Anybody home?"

The dogs approached, abject, base, sniffing my legs and shoes, cowering back in the weeds when I moved. Around the side of the house I found a couple of pickup trucks in what appeared to be working order (both had current licence plates) and a float, a flat aluminum boat with an airplane engine mounted on the back. These vehicles were used for crossing the swamps and muskeg in all seasons.

I smelled smoke and heard a beating noise, a hammering, from somewhere behind the house. The lane continued on behind an old garage, past the ruins of the barn, helter-skelter timbers atop a pile of rock and broken mortar, through a grove of thirty-foot sumacs, and into a low dip, what must have once been some kind of gravel pit. Here the collection of ruined cars was breathtaking; there must have been thirty of them, most of them twenty years old and more. In the midst of this graveyard, beside a shack, a rusty forge, and a welding tank, Donny Applewood pounded a piece of glowing metal with a hammer.

"Donny," I called out, "Donny Applewood?"

He turned. His face, though seamed, was still sallow beneath the grimy baseball cap. He was still skinny, except for his arms, which were sinewy with muscle.

He was expressionless. There was no sign of recognition.

"Ray Carrier," I said. "I used to live at the river farmhouse." I held out my hand. He wiped his on his pant leg. It was like shaking hands with an old shoe.

"I was in Merrick Bay for my father's funeral," I said.

"I heard," said Donny. He pulled out a pack of Exports, offered me one. The cigarette was strong and unfiltered, and the first few puffs made me dizzy. I looked around and felt I was in a foreign country.

"I saw your mother," I said.

He nodded.

"She was a client, a friend of my father's. Nice place she's in, the lodge."

"Don't get down there much," said Donny. He motioned to the yard, the piles of metal machinery, indicating what kept him here. The smoke from our cigarettes rose straight up from that inferno to the brilliant blue of the sky.

"I was hoping — I'd like to talk to your sister," I said. He just stood there staring at me. "You have her address?"

"Why?" he asked.

"I wanted to talk to her. Ask her a few questions."

"What questions?"

"Well, you know, my father, they found him at the edge of the bay with an old rowboat. I don't know if you'd remember — it was an old rowboat, had been a motorboat at one time, a disappearing propeller boat, before they took the engine out. Used to belong to one of the summer families, the Millers out on Providence Island?"

He scraped a fleck of tobacco from a tooth with a fingernail and spat on the ground.

"You know, your mother — your foster mother — she used to work out there at the island. I was hoping she might be able to tell me something about it — why my father might have been so interested in that boat. That's why I went down to the lodge — but your mother ..." I hesitated.

"Her mind's gone," said Donny.

"I'm sorry."

"Don't matter."

"I figured maybe Marj could tell me something. You know, mother, daughter, they were pretty close, weren't they? They talk."

He considered. Then he asked, "Why are you so interested in all this? You ain't trying to make trouble or something?"

"I won't make trouble. I'm just trying to find out ... well, what happened. My father died. I hadn't seen him in years, for a long time."

I paused for a moment. We finished our cigarettes.

"So, whatever happened to Bert?" I asked.

"In the penitentiary for a time, Kingston. Him and Spook, that Indian, Parry Sound ways. Killed some guy in a fight. Spook died in jail."

"What about Bert?"

"Lost track of Bert. Out west somewhere. British Columbia, last I heard."

He threw his cigarette on the ground and picked up the welding torch. From his pocket he took a flint lighter. Without looking up he said, "You go up to the house, get Mary Lou to give you Marj's address. Tell her I said so."

"Mary Lou?"

"My woman."

"I called when I was up at the house. Nobody answered."

"She's up there all right. Got a friend visiting. You must have seen the truck when you came in. You get up there, you just pound at the back door. We don't use the front no more."

He lowered his black goggles and flared the torch.

I walked back up the lane to the house. I banged on the back door. It was opened almost immediately.

"Hello, I was down talking to Donny —"

"I know. We saw you from the window. We seen your car come up."

"My name's Ray Carrier."

"We know who you are."

I explained about Marj's address.

"Sure, okay. Come on in. I'll get it."

The smell of the house was overpowering: a damp sweetness, and clothing and old food; the windows could not have been opened all winter. And it was hot. Despite the temperature outside, the wood stove in the corner burned; it was where they did their cooking.

I accepted a cup of tea. Mary Lou rummaged around in an old secretary desk, while her friend, sitting at the big table with her own cup of tea, looked on. She was a large woman. She twined a bit of hair in her fingers like a girl. She smiled at me, and there was something vaguely familiar in that smile.

Mary Lou found what she was looking for. She stood up with an envelope in her hand. She tore the flap from the envelope and handed it to me.

"There you are."

"M. Wilson," I read. The return address, in Cambridge, Ontario, was written in black ink.

"Sorry to hear about your dad. Clare here was just telling me. Funeral was up at the old church at the crossroads, right?"

I nodded. The jungle telegraph.

"So's your aunt, she going to stay on at the house?"

"I should think so." I drained the last of my tea. "Thanks for the tea, the address. I should be on my way."

The two of them followed me to the door. At the bottom of the outside steps I turned to say goodbye. But Mary Lou was turned toward the other woman; they spoke a few words, whispering. Mary Lou nodded at her friend. Could it have been Clarrisa, hidden under twenty years? Mary Lou came striding down the steps toward me, walking with a purpose.

"Come with me," she said.

I followed her across the yard to an overgrown path through a stand of aspen and young maples.

"Where are we going?" I asked her.

"Going to show you something. Don't tell Donny."

We tramped across a drying but still muddy field toward the old railway line. When I was a boy, we used to crouch beneath the culvert, waiting patiently (two trains daily) for the beast to thunder across, inches above our heads. There were no trains now. There weren't even any tracks; the railway companies had torn them up. We walked along the embankment. The ground was low and damp here. In the distance I saw the glitter of sun on water. Soon we were surrounded by swampland. Through the muskeg and dwarf pines, the poles of long dead trees pointed crazily toward the sky. We walked in silence, the rude growth swishing and catching at our ankles. I listened for the distant whistle of the train.

"There," she said, pointing to a kind of island, a patch of higher, flat ground in the middle of the muskeg. "They buried it out there."

"What?" I asked. When we were children, I used to imagine that this whole, poor countryside was haunted, and I saw now that it was.

"Donny and Bert, they put it there." She pointed once more. I was dizzy.

We stood there on the curve of the embankment of the abandoned railway, staring at that spot in the muskeg, the sun beating down on us, listening to the sound of frogs and insects and the whistle of the phantom train until it became unbearable.

| CHAPTER 24 |

"Too many hats," said Marjorie Applewood. "I wear too many hats."

She was speaking of how busy she was. She put away her briefcase. It was the big square kind that teachers and accountants carry, and poking out from the top I saw one of those green appointment books that teachers used. I felt a slight pang — the apprehension of the first day of class, that big book with our names in it on the teacher's desk. Or perhaps my apprehension was something else. Of course, I was nervous.

I'd picked her up at her school in a neighbouring village, a twenty-minute drive away. In less than an hour the first of her children would be home from their various schools and babysitters. She was fitting me in. And then there were the farm chores, the running of the house, and at seven o'clock, choir practice. These were the many hats.

"Not literally," she said, hanging up her raincoat, "although that, too, I guess, the cupboard's full of hats. Boots, too, all kinds of boots. Look." She laughed.

I looked, and it was true. The cupboard was a jumble of hats and coats and boots. And in the mudroom there was the rich smell of horse. She also gave riding lessons.

"We need lots of boots here. You can walk straight out the door and be in the countryside." She pointed out the open door to the meadow. I followed her into the main part of the house. "A bit like Merrick Bay," she said. "But the country here is different. More like England or France. Not that I've ever been to those places."

But I knew what she meant. The eastern side of the town, south of the highway, was encrusted with strip development. But then we had driven up a curving paved road from the centre of town, a street lined with Victorian houses and tall trees; at the top of the hill we turned a corner and were in the countryside, with barns and silos, and low hills stretching away into the distance, and the ribbon of the two rivers, the reason a town had been built here in the first place. Now I could see the river, broad and slow-moving, on the far side of the meadow. There were trees, shapely with dense, high canopies. I saw cattle underneath. Constable country. For Ontario it was a place that had been settled a long time, almost two hundred years. I had never been there before, but for the first time since I'd left Idaho, I felt as though I were home.

In the kitchen Marjorie's husband joined us. Eric. He was a teacher, too, high school music. He taught part-time; he also managed the farm and played in the Citizen's Band: the Dominion Day parade, concerts in the park, Boy Scout Day. He did it all for free. She had told me all this in the car. He was Scandinavian, he was tall, with a big, open face, and he spoke with a slight accent.

"Is the land good there?" he asked when he heard where I was from.

"Some of it's good," I said. The truth was I really didn't know. "Good for sheep farming."

He smiled. "That means it's not much good."

Marjorie offered to make us tea or coffee. "Or maybe Ray would like a drink," she said to Eric. "A beer or something."

The rooms were cool, a big stone farmhouse at the edge of town. Eric clumped down the cellar stairs and then back up again.

"No beer or wine," he said. "I'm sorry."

No alcohol in the house? This struck me as amazing. I took tea instead.

"How long have you been living here?" I asked.

"Eric and I have been living in this house for fifteen years, since just after we were married." They had met at teachers' college; she had told me this, too, in the car. "As for me, I've been living in this area since I left Merrick Bay. After my father died, I never felt that it was home. I'd been flighty."

I felt that I understood this perfectly. I remembered her father's death. It had made her more susceptible, more capable of being bruised, but it also made her more attractive. At sixteen years old, death had held for me a morbid fascination — it was impossible that we ourselves would ever die; death was a kind of romantic quality in others.

"You two will want to talk," said Eric. "I'll see to the horses."

As soon he left, there was an awkward silence. Marjorie still talked all the time, just as she always had. ("That girl was vaccinated with a gramophone needle," Phil Havelock's mother used to say.) She had talked in the car on the way here, but now that we had come to the reason for my visit, we were embarrassed. I stole glances at her as she sipped her tea, and I knew she was glancing at me when I looked away. Marjorie would have been in her late thirties that spring. She was bigger than she had been when she was sixteen, and not just taller. She had a more robust figure; when she was older, she would be stout, like her father. But she had the same dark hair, cut short almost like a cap, and the same large, dark, limpid eyes that she'd had as a girl. It was almost impossible not to look into her eyes.

"You look pretty much the same, Ray. Even those two lines around your mouth. You always had those. You look great, you know."

She laughed, looked down at her cup, then up again, and we were staring into each other's eyes. I wondered what she was thinking. No doubt she had thought about me, if even only in the two days since my telephone call. She had seemed reluctant to see me.

"We were just children then," I'd told her over the phone.

"We were still us."

"It was a long time ago."

"I remember what happened, and the feelings I had. I expect I will remember those things all my life."

I had told Marjorie that I had seen her mother and her foster brother, that I was in the area, and that I wanted to drop by. But she must have known there was more to it than that. I wondered whether she had judged me. I wondered whether she had forgiven me. I looked at her across the wooden table in her kitchen.

"Marjorie ..."

"Would you like some cake? Carrot cake, my mom's famous recipe. I should have asked you before. That long drive from the city. Would you like to stay for dinner?"

I declined the dinner but accepted the cake. Carrot cake. Homemade, with white sugary icing. She gave me a large piece.

"Do you still write poetry?" I asked.

And then she just started talking.

"I never write poetry now. I started writing poems a month or two after my father was killed in the accident. And I stopped, well, let's see, I stopped the following summer —" she paused "— when I started seeing Jack Miller. You know about that, I guess. Knew, I mean. That I was seeing Jack."

"Yes, I knew. Jack told me."

"He did? He told you? It was supposed to be this big secret. But Charmaine knew, of course, and Clare — you remember Clarrisa? — and I guess a couple of other girls. But my mother didn't know, not at first. At least I don't think she knew."

Her mother had warned her, of course; not just boys in general — although they were bad enough — but these summer people in particular. These rich Americans from the Bellisle Club. They liked to drink. They wouldn't take no for an answer. They thought they were God's gift. They thought they had the right because they were rich. "Well, we're just as good as they are," her mother had said.

But it hadn't been like that at all. It was much more complicated than her mother had ever made it seem. And also much more simple, like a sudden shining light.

"I'm surprised he told you," Marjorie said.

"I remember one time he wanted me to find out something, why you were mad at him, something like that. But why was it such a big secret?"

"I don't know, really. My mother didn't care for that family. She'd known them for years, and she didn't like them, ever since she was a girl. I guess she didn't like working for them, but we needed the money after my father died. That was part of it. Another thing, she used to go dancing with some of those people, years before."

"Dancing?"

"But Jack wanted it secret, too," she said, returning to the subject of her own past. "You know what I think now? This is terrible to say, but I think he didn't want his friends to know he was, you know, going out with some *farm* girl. I think he was ashamed."

From the kettle on the stove she poured boiling water to warm the teapot.

"I saw Quentin Miller, Jack's sister, a couple of days ago," I said. "Did you ever know her?"

"I never met her. In fact, I only ever even saw her a few times in my whole life. A couple of times at Ault's store, and then at that stupid party out at the farm, you remember that?"

"I remember."

"That was the first time I met Jack, me giving him hell for driving up on the lawn." She laughed, and there were lines on her face, too. And then she stopped laughing. "I guess I'll never forget that night."

She looked down, making circles on the table with her fingernail.

"I'll never forget it, either," I said.

The sound of a door slamming, footsteps in the mudroom, the first of her children arriving home: boisterous twins, a boy and a girl, and only five years old. They went to kindergarten in the morning and were picked up by the sitter in the afternoon. As if on cue, Eric came back into the kitchen. The children swarmed around him, clutching his legs. He picked up the girl. "You two come outside and help me. Your mum here has a visitor."

There was a constant passing of the load here, bantering and touching, a back and forth between Marjorie and Eric and the children and what had to be done. Happy families were like clubs. They made me feel excluded.

After the children had left the kitchen and gone to the front of the house, Marjorie poured us both more tea. She pushed the cake toward me.

"You liked that girl, Quentin?" She smiled and, reaching across the table, touched my wrist. "We were both a couple of idiots, though, weren't we just?"

"Why?" But I knew why.

"We liked each other. We were attracted to each other. And then we dropped each other like a couple of hot potatoes when the Millers came along. As if they were God's gift to the boonies. Funny — happened to both of us on the very same day." She removed her fingers from my wrist. "Their dad, he was making a run for the Senate or something? I remember there was a big fuss about that. Did he ever make it?"

I told her that he had lost. The last I'd read he was in the Betty Ford, some place like that, drying out.

"You ever get anywhere with her, Jack's sister?"

She evidently didn't know about the complicated marital arrangements, that Quentin was actually Jack's aunt, not his sister. I realized she'd hardly known the family at all. The Applewoods hadn't been up-to-date with the sort of information, what was common gossip elsewhere. "Sort of," I said. "Not really. Not exactly."

I wondered if, like Jack, Quentin had wanted to keep her relationship with me a secret because I was just a local. But there wasn't much to keep secret, and Quentin wouldn't have cared, anyway.

"Not like you and Jack," I said. "But if it was such a big secret, how did you ever see him? Did you see him often?"

"All the time."

"Where?"

"Where? Everywhere. He'd come up the creek in the canoe, sometimes in that old rowboat, or he'd drive and park on the back road by the black house. Then we'd walk and talk and — you know. In the barn. In the fields. Even in my room. He used to climb up on the front porch and in the window. He even climbed up a few times when my mother was in the house. It was very romantic. "Least it was to me."

"Did you ever go out to the island?"

"In all the time I lived in Merrick Bay, I was never out to the islands. I never went to that golf club place, either. Not once. I've never been in a summer cottage, to tell you the truth, at least not up there. Though I don't know why they call those places cottages. Funny when you think of it, me living up there all those years. The closest I ever got to working or playing with those people was helping out at Ault's store. That's when I first saw you. I never knew where to place you. When your dad bought that old river house, we all thought you were moving up year-round. You hung around with Phil Havelock and those guys, but you only came up in the summer."

But I didn't want to talk about me.

"Did you ever go to the pump house?" I asked. "You and Jack?"

"The pump house? That horrible place? Never. It was usually damp in there."

Abruptly, she stopped speaking. Her hand went to her mouth. She had gone pale. She stared at me.

| CHAPTER 25 |

She told me about telling Jack that she was pregnant, how hysterical he had become, how he stopped coming out to the farm, how he couldn't talk about it, seemed incapable of doing anything. Nobody knew. The days passed. The future was an abyss.

"Can't you visit some doctor or something?" Jack had asked one night as they walked behind the barn.

But nothing more was said about it, about that alternative or any other. They were immobilized.

Then, toward the end of the summer, something happened. There was a change. Jack's family found out. When Marjorie asked him how they knew, he said that he had told his father only after his father started asking him if he had something to tell him, almost bullying him.

I could picture this scene: Jack's father sitting him down in his office overlooking the verandah of the big house, the views down the lake.

"Now, is there something you'd like to tell me?" his father would have asked.

They would both be wearing their butter-coloured linen tennis clothing. "They already knew," Jack told her.

They guessed that Marjorie's mother must have told them. She'd found out — who knows how? It was certainly too early for anything to show.

One morning her mother had simply looked up at Marjorie at breakfast and said, "You're going to have a baby."

They wondered how she had known it was Jack when they had been so discreet. Perhaps Mrs. Ault had said something about Jack around the store. Perhaps Charmaine Ault had been less than discreet. This was something Jack and Marjorie never discovered.

But the others, they never found out that she was pregnant; Marjorie never told anyone that. The only people who knew were family, the Millers, Charmaine Ault. My father.

And then, after his mother found out, Jack changed his mind again. He said to Marjorie that they would have the baby together, after all, that he would stay up in Merrick Bay for the winter. They would live in the black house when the renters moved out at the end of the summer, fix it up. He would play hockey for Iron Falls to earn his money.

There would be a secret wedding.

Marjorie hadn't been thrilled and relieved and happy by this prospect, as he had expected. She understood that Jack didn't know what he wanted, or even what he was doing. He was like a yo-yo.

"What did you say to him?" I asked her.

"I said, 'Oh, Jack, yes. That will be fantastic.'"

But in the meantime, with her mother, she had put together an alternative plan ("the real plan," she said). It was a plan that grew almost without her and her mother having to speak about it; the pieces just seemed to fall into place. There was a relation in St. Thomas. A schoolteacher. No one in Merrick Bay knew her. And there was a place in St. Thomas that dealt with unmarried girls who had this sort of problem, a residence. She would go there.

It wasn't that she didn't trust Jack, that she didn't believe him, she told me. But you had to prepare for things; that was what her mother had said. Hope for the best in people, but plan for the worst.

She always felt cheated by all this. She'd read books about this sort of thing — summer romances with handsome visitors, sailboats glittering in the bay, skin kissed by the wind — but the stories never ended up in this kind of situation, and after only three or four weeks. She'd hardly gotten to know him and already she and her mother were discussing hiding and trips away to maiden aunts and the queasiness she was beginning to feel in the mornings. This was a different kind of reality altogether from the kind she had imagined would be her life in the stories and poems that she wrote.

And it was just as well that those plans had been made in the snippets of conversation she had with her mother, in those moments when they were hanging the laundry out to dry in the morning sun, or in the kitchen together after supper, or in the hall before bed. For in the fall, Jack's grandfather, J.D., found out and took an immediate interest in the matter. It was the year before his son, Jack Miller II, Jack's father, was to make his run for the Senate.

J.D. took Mrs. Applewood aside a few days before the Labour Day weekend. (I imagine his old man's tight claw on her elbow.)

"What's this I hear?" he asked. (I remember that he spoke with a slight rasp.) And when Marjorie's mother started to answer, he waved his hand, cutting her off. "Never mind. I have a plan."

"Does Jack know about the plan?" Mrs. Applewood had asked.

"Jack has gone," said J.D., "and don't you forget it."

The car would pick her up at the farm at nine o'clock in the morning and deliver her to the airstrip at Iron Falls. From there she would be flown to Boston. She would be in the clinic for two days; she would be back at school inside a week.

"What did you do?" I asked. "What did you and your mother tell him?"

It was past six now. The two older children had arrived home. Marjorie and I had moved from the kitchen into the front room. The tall sash windows were opened wide and the sheers fluttered in a light breeze from the south. In the kitchen, Eric had started the preparations for dinner; we could hear running water and the clatter of dishware.

"I couldn't decide," Marjorie said. "I — what's the word — I prevaricated."

She couldn't say yes and she couldn't say no. It wasn't so much a matter of principle as an unwillingness, an inability, to look to the future. She couldn't decide about anything.

"I didn't want to get on an airplane with that horrible old man. My mother wouldn't come with me."

Her mother wouldn't even discuss the plan with her. After the intervention of J.D., her mother sometimes seemed to have washed her hands of the whole matter, and she said things such as, "You're almost an adult now," and "If you're old enough to get into this kind of situation, you should be old enough to get out of it," and "Imagine that old man speaking to me like that."

Several times J.D. phoned.

And then one luminescent fall day in late September he arrived at the Iron Falls airstrip. Marjorie knew even before he telephoned her mother that he had arrived, because they saw the plane as it made high passes over Merrick Bay and the surrounding countryside. The plane glittered silver in the autumn sky.

That night she and her mother wept. Where was Jack? He had told her that he would be there. She didn't know how to reach him.

In the morning, Jack's grandfather phoned again. He said he would wait. By this time, she was eight weeks. The window was closing.

J.D. Miller took a room at the new Holiday Inn at Iron Falls. He phoned again the next day. He said that the Millers had rights in this matter, too. He reminded Mrs. Applewood that he had helped pay for her older son's art school in Toronto some years before. He hinted that there might be money if the appropriate course of action were followed. He wanted his grandson left alone to pursue his studies.

"Why can't he let the boy decide for himself?" Mrs. Applewood asked Marjorie when she was telling her of this conversation. "If Jack wants to come up here, he should let him."

"If he wanted to come, he would," said Marjorie.

J.D. was worried about his son's run for Congress, if this sort of news should come out. The timing was terrible. He hinted darkly at other things, influence he had, with the town council, with local banks. He demanded a meeting with Mrs. Applewood.

"What did you mother say?" I asked.

"She said that we weren't going to go along with the plan. She told him that he could meet with a friend of hers. Her lawyer."

I can only imagine what was said on the day of the golf game at the Bellisle Club — from the photo, from what Marjorie told me, from my aunt's story, and from what happened after. I know now that Mrs. Applewood had asked my father to approach J.D. Miller. She telephoned him in the city after she had already told the old man that my father would be there.

My father would have arrived at the golf club at around ten o'clock in the morning; I remember he'd left the city early. I see him wheeling into the empty parking lot under lowering clouds amid patches of blue sky — autumn weather in the lakes. J.D. Miller has already arrived. A man from the Merrick Bay garage had taken the big car out of storage and driven to the hotel at Iron Falls to pick him up. The car is drawn up by the great log portico at the side of the clubhouse. Off in the corner of the parking lot, Mrs. Applewood is waiting in the pickup. Donny is at the wheel.

When my father arrives, Mrs. Applewood hops out of the truck and walks quickly toward him. For some reason she has worn the outfit she always wore on Providence Island, the plain grey dress with the long skirt (although without the white apron) as though this might somehow count with the old man.

Standing there in the empty gravel parking lot, red and yellow leaves skittering across the gravel, she greets my father and talks to him before he meets J.D. All the Applewoods really want, she tells him, is to be left alone. It's a difficult enough situation as it is without this rich old man interfering. She wants Mr. Miller to back off, to fly away to America in his plane and not come back until next summer. No one will ever know, she says — people knowing is the last thing the Applewoods want. We don't want money. We don't want newspaper people; we don't want anything other than to be left alone. We will look after this matter. And if Jack wants to come to Merrick Bay to be with Marjorie, let him. Let the children be, because that's what they are.

I imagine that the Applewoods had started to think of J.D. Miller as some kind of devil who could sweep in on them whenever he liked in his airplane and his big black car, a malignant puppeteer. But when they met on the side lawn in front of the first tee where Mr. Miller was taking a cup of coffee with the manager, Mr. McVeen, everybody tried to be civil. There were pleasantries and conversation. And it was at this time that Mr. McVeen, fluttering because J.D. Miller was there, suggested taking a photo — the last game of the season, after all. After the game, the club staff would start taking down the pins. The caddy suggested taking the photo in front of the old Packard; you seldom saw a car like that outside a museum nowadays.

Then the game began. Mrs. Applewood waited in the lounge of the club. Donny said that he would walk into the village; he would be back in an hour and a half.

It must have been pleasant strolling those fairways with no other soul on the course. I could imagine the bracing air, the forests at the side of the course ablaze with colour, the lake that icy metal blue it seemed to take on as the cold weather came.

And what did my father say?

No doubt about what was legal and what was not. He was a great believer in the law. The law was a bulwark; without it there was chaos.

"That would be blackmail, Mr. Miller." He would not have to say more, to threaten to go the police; that would be self-evident. "This business of flying the girl to Boston. Such operations are illegal here. Are they not illegal in the United States?" He liked to make his points by asking rhetorical questions, or by making statements that seemed like questions. "I understand that your family is in the habit of making discreet contributions to local politicians." When he took a position, he was immovable. "We will resist any pressure that you bring to bear."

But I imagine he made his case mostly on the strength of his own virtue. My father was not a hard man, not some tough man who would stand an inch from J.D., grabbing his lapels and spitting in his face while he told him how it was going to be. Instead, he would reveal by his manner, by the way he spoke, by what he said, by the way he had lived his whole life, that some sorts of things weren't done. Some behaviour wasn't acceptable.

When they arrived back at the parking lot after the game, the back window of the limousine had been smashed. Mrs. Applewood looked at my father and Mr. Miller, bewildered. Donny was nowhere in sight.

"Who else could it have been?" asked Marjorie.

Mr. Miller drove away. There were no more phone calls. They didn't see him again.

I didn't ask Marjorie why she thought my father might have been pointing to the green rowboat the day he died; why, even knowing he had a heart condition, he had walked into the mud and then into that cold water to struggle with the boat. At first he had tried to push it free, as though he wanted it to sink back into the stinking water. I now see that this was perfectly consistent: of course, he would want it suppressed. And then he had wanted the boat brought ashore and destroyed by fire.

He had no illusions.

| CHAPTER 26 |

One morning in early May the following year, two months before J.D. Miller fell out of the green rowboat and drowned, Jack and Marjorie found themselves together once more in the scrabbly country behind the village of Merrick Bay. For them, for all of us, this would be the last summer at the lake.

"My grandfather is coming," said Jack. He was nervous. He had hidden his car behind the house.

"Your grandfather? Coming here?" said Marjorie.

They walked back from the black house toward the wooden drive shed at the back of the farmyard where they could talk in private; they knew that Mrs. Applewood and Donny and possibly Bert were somewhere nearby or in the house.

Bert was around, hiding in the woods all that spring and summer. "You remember," Marjorie told me. "I was afraid of him, but he was a friend of Donny's, and he sometimes had meals with us. My mother was a little vague about it, pretending she didn't know who he was. She didn't want to be helping a wanted criminal. But neither did she want to drive Donny away for good. And I guess she was a Christian; she believed in forgiveness. To a point."

But the place seemed just at that moment to be deserted, enveloped in silence. The dogs skulked around their legs. The small herd of cattle — several cows and their newborn young; all that was left to show for Mr. Applewood's years of effort — were pastured in a small field behind split rail fencing immediately beyond the shed. This was a detail that Marjorie particularly remembered, something she noted in her diary: the new life that seemed to be everywhere that spring, even in that bleak farmyard. Now she had the diary on the table in front of her as she told me the story.

"He doesn't know where we live," said Marjorie. "He doesn't know about me, about what happened. How can he be coming here?"

"He knows," said Jack. "He's coming."

"What for?"

"I don't know," said Jack.

After my father's visit the previous September to speak with J.D. Miller at the Bellisle Golf and Yacht Club, Marjorie and her mother had carried on with the original plan, the plan that had grown out of the air. Marjorie left the farm in the autumn to live with her aunt and to go to high school at a convent near St. Thomas, about two hundred miles southwest of Merrick Bay. At the convent there were several others in a similar situation to hers, which made Marjorie feel less lonely, less of an outcast than she might have felt otherwise, although none of them ever discussed their particular predicaments. She did well at school that year — at the convent they encouraged her in her work — and she learned how to play field hockey and even ice hockey, until her condition made that impossible. The time passed. The child, a baby girl, was born on May 1, and Marjorie returned to Merrick Bay when the school year ended. She brought the baby with her. This was unexpected, not part of the organic plan. She hadn't entirely made up her mind about whether to give the child up, but they were half thinking, Marjorie and her mother, even then, of keeping the child at the farm, of fabricating some story. They hadn't really thought about it, not formulated anything. That was the state of mind they were in when Jack told her that J.D. Miller was coming to the black house.

The only people in Merrick Bay who knew about the baby were Marjorie's family and Charmaine Ault. ("I always felt I was pretending," Marjorie told me, "with Jack, with my friends, with everyone.") But this kind of secret news — half good, half bad — was difficult to suppress. Perhaps people were starting to know. And now Jack Miller knew.

He had called her as soon as he arrived up at the lake that spring. He had volunteered to his father to come to Providence Island early to oversee the opening of the house. He hadn't known what had happened; with threats and money and who knew what force and enticements, his family had kept him away all winter, despite his declarations to Marjorie of the summer before. Now he was back. He had called her; they had met for coffee once in the Bay Café. He had been rather distant, and for Marjorie this meeting confirmed once and for all that there would never really be anything more between them.

She told him then that she had gone ahead and had a baby. Jack had said nothing. He hadn't come out to the farm for several days, not until this June morning. To warn her that his grandfather was descending like a great black bird.

The Packard had been exhumed from the garage behind the Merrick Bay Hotel for the second time in less than a year. Over the winter the rear window had been replaced, the car polished, and cleaned inside and out.

The Applewoods imagined that J.D. might alight with his money and power and take the child away. They wanted no part of him. And so, whatever his motives, they determined he would never see the child.

"When is he coming?" Marjorie asked.

"Now. He's on his way."

They fled from the house. Marjorie held the baby in her arms. They ran across the lower field toward the stream. They reached the stone pump house, hidden in the stand of willows. It must have seemed a sanctuary.

The Applewoods had several wells and also the creek, which brought runoff and spring water down from the hills and forest. Sucker Creek was stained bloody by the tamarack swamps, but it was good water all the same. The pump house hadn't been built to bring water in, but rather to pump it out. The fields there were low and wet, and some ancestors (Alpenvord had been their name then) had hoped to find rich dark soil for making a market garden; Dutch settlers had done that in the Holland Marsh a hundred miles to the south. But the soil was poor, and once the banks of Sucker Creek had been built up and fields drained, there had been little need to use the pump house again. The fields were used only for summer pasture, when they were dry, and then not at all.

"We'll leave the baby in here," Jack said.

"No," said Marjorie.

"We'll leave the baby here."

"No, no, we can't do that." She was yelling a little now, aware that she was becoming hysterical. "The water, the water might come up," she said.

"What are you talking about?" asked Jack. "Spring thaw is over. Look." He strode a step or two up the incline and pulled her by the hand. They looked over the bank. The river ran swiftly, but it was well below the top of the bank. "The river is perfectly safe."

"Jack, this baby is only days old."

When she had met Jack Miller, he had been so charming, his voice, his manners, the way he wore his tennis sweater knotted by the sleeves around his neck. But now he wasn't charming. He wasn't languid or easy. He was a panicky, red-faced child, afraid of what he'd done, afraid of his family. Afraid especially of J.D.

"It'll only be for half an hour," said Jack. "We'll come right back and get her as soon as he's gone."

It was dark in the pump house and warm from the morning sun. And perhaps it seemed even darker to them after the green and yellow light outside. They didn't notice the beginning of something stirring, nor the dark depression in the floor in the corner of the room. They might have also heard a silken slithering in the tall grass around the house, a creeping away, but they were excited and in a hurry.

They put the baby in swaddling blankets in a basket on the day bed in the middle of the room. Then they returned to the black house.

Donny and Bert hid in one of the upstairs bedrooms behind dirty lace curtains, watching the old man approach.

Mrs. Applewood and Marjorie waited. I imagined them primly dressed, standing beside one another in the empty front parlour — they never had much in the way of furniture, and what there was had been old and worn.

Jack, I saw, sweating a few steps behind, watching the big car come up the drive, a cloud of dust rising in the air behind.

J.D. was alone. The car had been fitted with special hand controls so that it could be driven by him without use of the pedals, but J.D. Miller virtually never ventured anywhere without help, his driver, Mrs. Applewood, a member of the family, or a servant. Today he was alone. That was something.

They heard the car door slam shut with a metallic thunk. Then the barking of the dogs as they surrounded him, snarling and feinting. The Applewoods didn't receive many visitors; when they did, Donny customarily materialized from somewhere and took control of the dogs. Not this time. No one moved.

But J.D. wasn't a man to be intimidated by mere black dogs. He struck the largest hard across the top of the head with his black cane; the dog yelped and rolled away in terror. The other two followed, slinking away toward the bushes at the side of the lane.

They heard his footsteps on the hard ground, the drag of his bad foot, and then the rap of his cane on the front steps. They saw his looming shape at the door, a black shadow on the curtains.

Marjorie let him in. It was the first time they had ever met. He ignored her. He looked up, and his eyes caught Jack's. He froze for a moment; this wasn't what he had expected. He turned to Mrs. Applewood.

"Alice, I thought you would be alone."

Alice?

"Using her name like that," Marjorie said to me, "that told all. They had been lovers years before. Perhaps not so long before." She understood why her mother's feelings about J.D. and the Millers had been so strong. And she understood, too, that Jack had known this all along — a rollicking family legend.

They stood silent for a moment, waiting for him to say something more. It seemed to Marjorie as though he were listening for something, the sound of the child perhaps. And they did hear something, a shuffling from the upstairs of that small frame house. Noise carried easily there.

J.D. looked up at the dark wooden ceiling. "Who's up there? Tell me."

Mrs. Applewood called out, "Donny. Donny, come down here."

Donny Applewood. He would have been wearing his customary dirty black jeans and dark T-shirt, the cigarette pack tucked in the sleeve. He came down the wooden stairs and continued on through the room. At first Marjorie thought he wasn't going to speak at all, but before he reached the door he turned to Jack and said, "You brought him here."

When Donny had left the room, J.D. Miller asked, "Is there an infant in this house?"

"No," said Marjorie.

Mrs. Applewood said nothing.

"Where is it?"

("That's what he called the baby," Marjorie told me. "It.")

This time Mrs. Applewood spoke. "I have no idea what you're talking about."

"Don't be ridiculous, Alice. We all know what was going on last fall — you had that lawyer from Toronto come up here and as good as threaten me. We all know what we were talking about. I want to know what happened in the end. I have a right."

"J.D.," said Jack, "I can look after this."

"Don't be ridiculous. You can't look after anything."

"But —" Jack began. J.D. motioned him silent with a wave of his cane. "You go upstairs, see if the child is up there — go on, boy, do as I say."

Jack did as he was told. He was back downstairs in a moment.

"Nothing," he said, averting his eyes from the old man and toward the floor.

"Tell me what happened," said J.D. "I understand the child was born, that the child is here."

Marjorie turned to Jack. "Did you tell him?"

"It had nothing to do with him," said J.D. To Jack he said, "Go back and look again!" And to Marjorie: "We had a detective. A fellow from Rochester. He drove up to that town you were staying in. All that is neither here nor there. If we could find out, so could others. We need to decide what to do next. Give me the baby. I'll look after everything. These things have happened before, you know. You're not the first. I can take care of it. We all want what's best."

"Would the baby have a good home?"

Marjorie remembered having asked him that. Perhaps she was looking around the shabbily furnished room where they stood when she said it, or thinking of the rusty red pump that supplied the water to the kitchen sink. Or the old stone pump house.

The old man had been speaking to Mrs. Applewood. Now he turned to Marjorie. "A good home? Of course. Schools, good clothes, everything. And no one will ever know." He smiled.

"No!" said Mrs. Applewood. She held her hands clasped tightly in front of her.

Mr. Miller turned away from Marjorie and glanced at Mrs. Applewood, surprised at the strength of her response.

"Get out of here," Mrs. Applewood said. "Leave my home this instant."

"Your home?" said J.D. He turned, pivoting on the cane. "Fine, we'll go." He jabbed the cane in the air, pointing at Jack. "You — come with me."

Jack hesitated for only a moment. He preceded his grandfather out the door, but on the front stoop he turned and gazed at Marjorie.

It was a helpless look, Marjorie told me. After all, what could he do?

"I'm sorry, Marj." Jack smiled. It was that old smile. I knew it well.

She never saw him again.

Mr. Miller left the house in silence.

The baby was alone in the pump house for half an hour.

| CHAPTER 27 |

I don't remember exactly how or when this particular death first came into my consciousness in the way that it did. The story I was always telling myself, the story that for over twenty years had had no ending, had its beginnings with my aunt and my father discussing some newspaper story. This was the autumn after my job at Confederated Paving had ended. I was home from university for the weekend.

"Horrible," my aunt had said. "What kind of people would do such a thing?"

"These things sometimes happen in rural communities," my father said. "In India, in China, infanticide has been practised for years." Yet I remember that he seemed uneasy to me. He seemed unnaturally interested in calming us. I had never heard him comment before about the lurid stories in newspapers. None had ever happened so close to home.

"We are not India or China," said Aunt Beth. "This is Ontario. A Christian country."

It was then that my dreams of snakes began. There was something in the air: what my father knew, and what I feared.

"Ray, are you all right?" my father asked. "You look a little green about the gills."

They both stared at me across the breakfast table.

Marjorie knew something was wrong the instant she heard the dogs. The yelping. She and her mother still stood side by side on the front stoop from where they had watched the two cars disappear. The dust settled in the high grass at the side of the road. She was wondering what they would do now that J.D. and Jack Miller were gone, both of them gone; she was wondering what would happen to their lives now, when the barking came, breaking the silence that had descended as the cars' engines faded, as though it were awaking them from a dream.

The noise of the dogs came from the direction of the river.

Marjorie walked through the front room. She seemed to float. Time slowed. It was as though she were drugged. She took the large black umbrella from the coat cupboard. She meant to chase the dogs with it; she had seen the umbrella used in that way before. She looked out the kitchen window and saw them: one moment the dogs were on their haunches, retreating, jaws flashing pink and white, the next they were up again, advancing and running back, approaching the door of the pump house, darting and feinting, frenzied.

It was as if they had cornered something. A rat or a weasel, that was what she thought at first, some animal loose in the pump house with the baby. She ran across the field. The weeds scratched her legs. In some places, her feet sank in because the field was still damp. She yelled as she ran; she had some idea of scaring away the animal, whatever it was, along with the dogs. She'd almost arrived at the pump house when she slipped, something underfoot, the squish of the mud, and she fell. A slithering, skittering away; whatever had tripped her was gone. She was on her feet again in an instant. At the door of the pump house, she flailed at the dogs with the umbrella.

The room was small, perhaps eight feet square, with the old day bed from the Eaton's catalogue taking up most of one wall. The crib was on the day bed. It was almost noon; the sun was higher in the sky now and she could see better than she had been able to in the morning. The light filtered through the leaves of the willows and shimmered yellow green. She couldn't tell what it was that was happening in there. She thought at first it was water from the river, after all: green-and-brown water, oily sludge, spilling down onto the mud floor from the two small windows. But there was something wrong; the current was going the other way, not down the walls, but up. And so thick, like a carpet. What kind of river was this? A noise like a river, a steady seamless rustling.

And then she saw.

The floor was alive.

Snakes.

Marjorie screamed. She beat at the floor with the umbrella. Each time she raised her arm to strike again, the umbrella was festooned with snakes. They fell at her feet. She threw the umbrella to the floor. She reached across the room and snatched the baby. The crib and the day bed were a seething mass of snakes. She grabbed the baby. The baby was twelve days old — pink and swollen flesh. She brushed the baby to remove the snakes. A snake fell from the baby's mouth. The baby was still and quiet. She held the baby tightly to her chest, and she ran across the field the way she had come. From the backyard, beneath the clothesline, her mother watched, one hand to her mouth in disbelief. Marjorie ran into her mother's outstretched arms. She leaned into her mother, sobbing. The infant in her arms was still and quiet.

They put the baby back in the crib and placed the crib in the upstairs bedroom. All that day and night they wept.

"No one knows," Mrs. Applewood kept saying.

On the morning of the following day, Donny and Bert came into the kitchen. They were hot and dirty. It was still dark outside, pearly grey. Marjorie and her mother had both been sleeping, on the two ragged chesterfields in the front room.

"It's okay," said Donny.

Mrs. Applewood gazed at her foster son. It was if she were asking a question.

"We looked after it," said Donny.

"The baby's gone," said Bert.

Perhaps Marjorie and her mother realized that for Donny it was his chance. His chance to do something.

Bert said, "It's not a crime to bury your own dead."

"Some fishermen found it," Mary Lou had said to me that day in the muskeg, pointing out beyond the abandoned rail bed. "Looking for bait, frogs and crayfish and such. Only flat dry place around here, so naturally they headed for it. Was in a shallow grave, like, with some other garbage? Stupid thing for them to do, putting it there. Animals had gotten into it, I guess. Anyways, they found it."

The Applewoods said a prayer.

Afterward, Donny said, "No one needs to know about this."

And no one ever did know. Even when the body of the baby was discovered two months later, found by those fishermen out in their airboats looking for bait, dug up and half-eaten by animals. An image flashed in my mind: Mr. Havelock slaughtering the calf, the flash of the blade, the blood from its throat, the mass of glistening innards. Bile rose in my throat.

The body of a baby girl was found in a green garbage bag in the muskeg near the edge of the endless forests in the spring of 1966.

Marjorie Applewood had one of the yellowed news clippings folded in her journal:

> The infant was at first supposed to have died of injuries suffered during a beating. Death was later determined to have been caused by snake bites, possibly rattlesnake bites ... the police have made inquiries at hospitals throughout the district ...

No one even came to see the Applewoods.

("I sometimes wish they had," Marjorie told me. "Sometimes I wish it had all come out. That people knew, or admitted that they knew.")

But there was one other person who already knew there was a new baby girl in the world. There was one person Mrs. Applewood would have to tell. There was one person who would have to pay. And there was one person who would have to keep the knowledge of these events in his heart.

CHAPTER 28

Over lunch I fell into conversation with a man at the bar in the Merrick Bay Hotel. I told him that as a boy I had spent my summers here, that I used to play tennis on the red clay courts on Providence Island. Now a friend had offered to take me over and show me around the place again one last time. This was a couple of days after returning to Merrick Bay from my trip to see Marjorie Applewood, and almost two weeks after my father's funeral.

"Providence Island? The big house over there? You know it's been abandoned for years? Hey, you ever heard the story about that place? There was this old man over there. Years ago. Fell out of a rowboat and drowned. They were rowing off the bluffs on the far side, see, him and his nursemaid? She hits him over the head with an oar and pushes him out of the boat."

Outside, the whine of an outboard motor, the beginnings of the summer season on Merrick Bay.

"Wonder why," I said.

"I guess she just liked smashing things," said the man at the bar, "like people's heads."

He laughed. We each took a sip of our beers. The bartender listened in.

To the people of Merrick Bay, the disappearance of J.D. Miller the day of the regatta twenty-three years before was more than an accident but less than history. It was local colour. A tale told with relish. But to my father it had been something more, a truth, and a secret that he had kept until the very end. I wondered how he had reacted over the years as the story had gained currency, hearing people tell it as they stood around the counter at Ault's store, in the local bars, over drinks.

And that poor woman (they would have said in the earliest versions), Mrs. Applewood, who had been with him — in a way it was her fault, and she'd never been the same since. But as the years passed, the story changed. Mrs. Applewood lost her name; she became the nursemaid, the housekeeper, and then simply the woman in the boat. And the reasons, the sequence of events behind the accident, they changed, too, depending on the time, perhaps on the mood and the personal history of the teller. In the earliest versions, closest to the time when it happened, J.D. insisted that he be taken out, as he always insisted he be taken out in the boat, even though it was rough and he was a cripple. He was imperious, and these things happened.

Then it became a story of sudden passion: "He tried something in the boat. He had it coming, the old goat." (People could no longer remember the old man, but they knew that he had been rich and powerful, that he had once married a movie star.) And, finally, a carefully planned assassination: "She always rowed him around the island. She was biding her time. There had been something between them. She was just waiting for the right opportunity."

I imagined my father hearing the stories, smiling with the others as they were told. The people of Merrick Bay weren't unhappy to have the Millers, to have this tale of passion and murder to tell. This thirst for scabrous tales about the rich, the local flavour, made it all that more appealing

"That nursemaid, who was she, anyway?" asked the bartender.

"Who knows?" said the man at the bar. He had moved to Merrick Bay ten years before.

These kinds of questions must have come up for years.

When I saw the hole in the bottom of the boat, it was clear to me at least that the drowning was no accident, that all these rumours and stories had something to them. I thought I knew what my father had been pointing at that morning in May. It didn't matter whether what he'd seen was the body, the ghost, of J.D. Miller or not. He thought he had. And when he made his way through the mud of the bay, only the green rowboat was there.

The bartender brought my sandwich.

The pump house was in my dreams, my nightmares, but the people here told the story with a smile. Teenagers on the lake called the big house on Providence Island the haunted house, just as we used to call the Allen place the haunted house. They went there for sex. They lit bonfires on the patch of long grass behind the main dock where the lawn used to be kept like a golf green, and where the big blue-and-white awning had been set up the day of the seventy-fifth anniversary party.

"Some guy is supposed to have seen a body out there," said the man at the bar, glancing out the window toward the islands in the distance. "How do you figure — would that be good for the tourist trade, to play up this kind of thing? Or would it scare them away?"

"Maybe the body wasn't him," said the bartender. "Maybe it was the Indian. From the lagoon."

"You know everything," I said.

"I ought to. I'm the mayor around here."

I asked him if he knew Phil Havelock.

"Of course."

"And this development they're proposing? The condominiums. Is it going through?"

"You can count on it. There's money on the table. You want to see the place, you better get out there soon."

I paid for my beer and sandwiches and walked along the shore road to the bottom of the bay. The bulldozers were back at work filling in the swamp at the mouth of Sucker Creek. There was a large iron barge tethered to the shore, and on top of this another yellow machine, a backhoe. Tied to the barge was a pontoon boat with an awning and a couple of big outboards on the back. Phil waved. There were five others on the boat with him. They all wore business suits. Prospective buyers and the real estate agent who had arranged the charter.

"Come aboard," he said. "We'd almost given up on you."

As soon as I was aboard, Phil started the motors and the mouth of Sucker Creek receded behind us.

The low buildings of the town, the pine trees along the shore, and the dark green humps of the island were edged with a luminous glow. Not a breath of wind: the lake was a sheet of glass.

By the submerged cribs of the old steamboat pier, Phil slowed the boat. The water had now risen above the tops of the cribs, but you could still see the immense timbers, rocks, and rusty spikes a few inches below the water. Around the cribs the depth of the lake was almost twenty feet.

"Great fishing over these old pilings," Phil said.

He revved the motors, and we continued down the shore of the island. At the mouth of the lagoon, Phil stopped the engines and the real estate agent began his pitch. The lagoon was to be sheathed in docking; there would be a multi-slip boathouse and rows of plastic outboards bobbing along beside. "This is where we put the gas pumps, the new marina, the condo club house. A natural harbour." We continued on down the shore toward the boathouses.

Much that I had seen on the trip lately had seemed smaller than I remembered — the town, the landscape and the abandoned farm buildings, the people — but Providence Island appeared to be larger. It was an illusion created by the lack of care; the buildings seemed to loom up out of the overgrowth. The shadows of the boathouses made the water black, and there was darkness, too, in the yawning gaps of the doors. The paths along the shore, once neatly groomed, were overgrown with weeds and the low branches of trees.

"Why are they selling the place?" I asked. "Do they need the money?"

"Of course, they need the money. Who doesn't? Besides, nobody uses the place anymore. Jack hasn't been up in years. The other brother is dead. The parents are divorced."

We continued up the hill. Vandals had been here before us. There were empty beer bottles, garbage, and evidence of dogs. I looked up at the crumbling stone steps that led to the plateau, to the two ponds and the wooden water tower. I wondered if the whole romantic past that I had burnished in my memory had even existed. I asked about the water tower.

"Collapsed," said the real estate agent. "We flew over in a plane the other day to take some pictures. Saw it from the air. I guess some kids pushed it over."

The tennis court was gouged and scarred. Some of the weeds growing through the surface were two feet high. The fencing at the ends was rusted through.

The real estate agent pointed to a thin stream of smoke coming from one of the back chimneys of the house. "The nerve of these kids. Someone's been in there and lit one of the fireplaces."

The house was partially shuttered — all the upstairs windows and most on the ground floor — but the verandah doors were open, the screens had begun to rot, and the front door was partially opened.

Phil called out, "Hello? Anybody here?" Silence. Someone had been in the house the night before, but we had seen no boats at the docks and we were alone now. Above the musky smell of dampness and old furniture there was the wisp of a scent of a wood fire.

In a corner of the front hall I saw the red leather guest book on the lectern opened to 1915, the year Woodrow Wilson had been a guest. The paper was yellow, the script faded brown. I flipped ahead to the night of the party when Quentin had asked me to sign.

There was a loud noise, like a shot ringing out.

"Is everything okay?" one of the buyers asked.

"You stay here," Phil said to the agent and the others. "Ray and I will have a look."

We checked the fireplaces in the main rooms. But it wasn't one of the fireplaces. It was the wood stove in the kitchen. You could feel the heat from halfway across the room. On top of the stove was broken glass, an unopened beer bottle that had shattered from the heat.

It was difficult to see; the only light came from between the cracks of the shutters.

"Let's open the windows," Phil said. "Let some light in here."

I raised the sash of the big window beside the stove, unhooked the shutter, and pushed. The shutters wouldn't budge.

Phil came over to give me help. We both pushed. With a crack, the shutters opened, but the whole side of the kitchen shuddered, and the metal chimney at the back of the stove came tumbling down, spewing more billowing white smoke into the room. Flames licked out the back of the stove. With a whoosh the fire leaped to the ceiling.

We worked hard, almost frantically, trying to save what we could. We carried things from the main rooms: paintings and fading photographs and papers from desks and the drawers of tables in the front rooms. We even carried out a few pieces of furniture. But the back of the house was filling with smoke, and the temperature was rising. We could hardly breathe.

Phil and I found a couple of ancient fire extinguishers hanging on the wall near the wood stove: tear-shaped glass containers about the size of a cantaloupe, each filled with clear red liquid that looked like cream soda. They shattered and steamed when we threw them at the flames; the liquid dribbling down the walls. But the curtains were on fire by then and the flames licked along the ceiling; the paint shrivelled in pieces and fell to the floor in curling white strips.

From the nook behind the staircase in the front hall I'd called the fire department at Merrick Bay. There was a large metal fire extinguisher there, too, the kind you turn upside down to activate. I hauled it to the kitchen. But the heat was too intense. The fire began to roar like a freight train. A wind rose, sucking air into the back rooms.

By the time the fireboat came from farther up the lake, with its pumps and hoses, the walls of the upper storeys of the house, the turrets and balconies, had already begun to collapse. The firemen turned their hoses on the trees and bushes around the house to keep the fire from spreading to the forest — although it was unlikely that the trees would burn at this time of year — and to prevent sparks from igniting the boathouses and other buildings.

As darkness fell, I could feel the heat out on the lake from hundreds of feet away, and the flames reached high into the sky. The light prevailing wind carried the smoke east over the village of Merrick Bay.

| CHAPTER 29 |

The snakes were striped yellow-green and black. I woke with a start in the darkness of the early morning and thought for a moment that Katie was in the bed beside me, that I was in her house in the foothills, the trees tall in the moonlight where the road turned rough as the valley broadened, a barn and a few fields rising behind and into the forest and the clear night sky. The pillow smelled of smoke.

I pulled on a gown and crept downstairs to the kitchen. Fine ash was still falling in the garden like the first snow. I picked up the phone and dialled the number.

"I'm coming home," I said.

"Did you find out what you wanted to about your father's death?" Katie asked. I said that I had. She seemed hesitant to ask more, as if perhaps she already knew enough. Then she said, "Those old rowboats, that old man's death, your father's death, were they connected, do you think?"

I gazed out the kitchen window to the curve in the river that made the pool where we used to swim, the tire on a rope that we used to swing out into the water, the weedy lawn between the house and the river where Phil and I once played catch. We would walk up the path through a stand of white pines behind the house to the pink granite plateau from which my father and I watched the Northern Lights, the forests stretching away to the north, and looking east, derelict farmland: our place, the Havelocks', the Applewoods', the river snaking away beyond the tamarack swamp.

"You didn't answer," she said, "about your father and that old man."

"All three deaths were connected," I said.

"What was the third?"

"You remember the story — I'm sure I've told you — the baby that was found in the woods."

"You read about those stories from time to time. Teenagers, hillbillies, they have the baby and they don't know what to do. No, I don't remember."

The day after the fire I drove to the lodge, the retirement home. I didn't know whether Mrs. Applewood could understand me, but I wanted to tell her, anyway; it was a way of making a narrative of these events to myself as much as to her. A closing.

I told her that I had seen Marjorie, that I had seen Donny.

"He was a good boy, Donny. Not much here, though." She touched her head. "You don't have to tell me that. But a lot here." She touched her chest. "Always looking out for his sister."

I told her I knew now about the baby. "It was an accident," I said.

"It didn't seem like an accident at the time," she said. Then she smiled. "Just like the accident Mr. Miller and I had by the old steamboat cribs!"

She wouldn't have needed to strike him with any oar, any cane, the way he had struck the dogs. She wouldn't need to row around to the rough water and push him out. She just had to row the boat onto the crib, ease herself overboard, and swim ashore.

"You walked across the island to where I found you?"

"You? You found me? Found me out? Is that it?" She went blank again. She turned and looked out the window. The maple and beech trees were bowing to us in the greenness of summer; it had happened in a matter of days, the leaves coming, that same miracle year after year. I followed her gaze to the open window. The light was dazzling.

I rose to leave. I put my hands on her shoulder. She turned to look at me.

"My father never told a soul," I said. I didn't say he had died trying to protect her.

Aunt Beth stood on the front porch, her hair wispy in the breeze. She had stood there watching while I loaded the luggage. She waved as I pulled out of the drive. I drove up the river road again. I was intoxicated. After the fire, the air seemed unnaturally clear and sweet.

In Merrick Bay the water level had returned to normal. All the debris that had been there was washed away.

ALSO BY GREGOR ROBINSON

The Dream King
978-0-88873-877-6
$16.95

With exceptional power, Gregor Robinson exposes both the gravity and levity of relationships — formed in duty, in fear, in need — and the subtle ways we attempt to escape their persistent pull. At turns humorous, chilling, and tender, Robinson's short fiction displays a versatility in tone and subject that mirrors the stories of our lives, real or imagined, domestic or exotic. His writing elevates the "What If?" to new imaginary heights.

OTHER GREAT FICTION FROM DUNDURN PRESS

Six Metres of Pavement
by Farzana Doctor
978-1-55488-767-5
$22.99

Ismail Boxwala made the worst mistake of his life one summer morning twenty years ago: he forgot his baby daughter in the back seat of his car. After his daughter's tragic death, he struggles to continue living. A divorce, years of heavy drinking, and sex with strangers only leave him more alone and isolated. But Ismail's story begins to change after he reluctantly befriends two women: Fatima and Celia, his grieving Portuguese-Canadian neighbour who lives just six metres away. Each makes complicated demands of him, ones he is uncertain he can meet.

Something Remains
by Hassan Ghedi Santur
978-1-55488-465-0
$21.99

Andrew Christiansen is having a bad year. His mother has just died, his father gets arrested, and he's married to a woman he doesn't love. To make matters worse, Sarah, the gifted actress from his past, storms back into his life, bringing with her the possibility of happiness. Keeping Andrew sane is his beloved camera and his friendship with Zakhariye, a Somali-born magazine editor grieving the death of a son. *Something Remains* probes the various ways humans grieve when the lives they build for themselves fall apart. It speaks of the joy we find in what remains and the hope that comes with life putting itself back together in ways we never imagined.

Available at your favourite bookseller.

What did you think of this book? Visit www.dundurn.com for reviews, videos, updates, and more!